SHE WON'T LEAVE

A gripping psychological thriller

James Caine

Copyright © 2024 James Caine

All rights reserved

The characters and events portrayed in this book are fictitious. Any similarity to real persons, living or dead, is coincidental and not intended by the author.

No part of this book may be reproduced, or stored in a retrieval system, or transmitted in any form or by any means, electronic, mechanical, photocopying, recording, or otherwise, without express written permission of the publisher.

DOWNLOAD MY FREE BOOK

If you would like to receive a FREE copy of my psychological thriller, 'The Affair', email me at jamescaineauthor@gmail.com

PROLOGUE

Delores

I was married for over forty-six years, until today.

Leonard and I may have had a long marriage, but none of it was the type of romance writers would describe. Our relationship didn't start with a bang, but it certainly ended with one.

I would like to say that we were happy together. In our defense, a few of the many years we shared were, possibly the ones where we were new to each other – but even those weren't amazing, to be honest.

Mediocre at best.

The powerful Leonard Sterling hated mediocrity, which seemed ironic when I think of our marriage. No matter how much money, land, or success he accumulated in his life, our marriage remained hollow.

I stare at a picture of us in our massive living room. The room shares dark features illuminated by the sunlight that pours through towering windows, casting a warm glow, highlighting the expensive furniture and drawing the eye to the large fireplace with its marble mantle.

We had everything in life anyone could ever want. A large, ridiculously expensive house. Maids, chefs, gardeners... People would believe that our life was as majestic as this beautiful home. No matter what expensive things we put in this house, this portrait of us never seemed to fit.

The picture of the "happy" couple, Leonard and Delores Sterling. We had a professional photographer take it for us a few years ago upon my request.

Leonard didn't care for it. He rushed me that day to get ready. He refused to go to the photographer's studio. He would only accept it being taken at our house or his office, where it was convenient for him to be available.

So we had the photographer take our photo of us in our home, in the living room. The same living room I stand in now.

Leonard sat in his favourite leather chair. I stood beside the chair, my hand on his shoulder. Even in pictures, we seemed so distant. No romantic embrace even for the small moments a camera lens can capture. We couldn't even pretend to be in love for the photographer.

Leonard demanded the photographer hurry and take the picture so he could return to his work. The man did as requested. One shot. That was all Leonard would allow. He gave me what I wanted. A picture of us hanging in our home. It's the only one of us in this house.

Instead of leaving to go to his precious office, Leonard took out a large cigar from his suit jacket. He lit it and sat in his favourite chair as the photographer dismantled his set-up.

We could have easily taken more pictures together. Maybe we could have pretended to be happy.

It never made sense why we couldn't have been. I was the perfect wife to my husband. I took care of my body, not letting age get the best of me. I threw myself at the man willingly, but he could care less, only willing to touch me on anniversaries or random nights for minutes of pleasure.

I was willing to be anything for my husband.

If a stranger was to walk inside my home and rummage around, they would have no clue who owned it, with this picture being the only evidence to support it was us. Leonard found it tacky to hang pictures of us on the wall, but I didn't care. Even he wouldn't stop me from putting pictures of my darling son, Leo, on the walls. I suppose the strangers who entered would assume that the small boy somehow owned this mansion.

We named Leo after his father, but my boy shares no characteristics of my husband. Caring, loving and always smiling, Leo is perfect.

Although my sweet boy's face reminds me of the love I still have in my life, he has grown much older now. He's become a businessman himself, much like his father. Unlike my husband, my son still attempts to have me involved in his life, even though it's less than I like.

Even when Leo realized what a wretched person his father was, my son still kept in contact with me, although it wasn't much. I was worried after their falling out that it would be the end of the only relationship in my life worth having.

Thankfully, that wasn't the case for a long time, until somewhat recently.

My son is married. He was naive, young and supposedly in love. In love enough to marry someone nearly as wretched as his father. He just doesn't see it that way.

His wife, Madelyn, may be sweet as pie, but she

doesn't have the background to deserve my son. She had nothing before my boy came into her life. She sank her claws into my son until he agreed to marry her.

Just like his father, she keeps me away from my son, but I won't allow her to do that any longer. My son has moved into a large house close to mine in Summer Hills. It's a small community in northwest Calgary where many of the wealthiest live. This should be an opportunity for us to see each other more, but I know she won't allow it.

He is my blood. She's the outsider.

It took me years to realize the mistake I made being with my husband. I hope I can help my son realize his error much sooner.

I pause a moment, staring at the picture of Leonard and me again.

I hung it in the same living room where the picture was originally taken. Part of me wanted it here to remind myself how infuriating it was being with a man like Leonard Sterling. To remind myself that he had all the power. He got what he always wanted.

I look over at my husband in the living room. He's still sitting in that chair. Instead of the expensive cigar being held tight in his mouth, it's dropped to the floor by his foot, embers still glowing. On the side table beside him is a rock glass with expensive scotch, his reading glasses, and a typewritten note left behind.

I light my own cigarette and enjoy the taste as I inhale.

Just as I did in the portrait, I stand behind my husband, placing my hand on his shoulder. I peer at the side of his head, where the bullet entered his skull. His body is slumped to one side, and his cold eyes are wide.

As I exhale, a plume of smoke covers my husband's

face.

As much power as Leonard Sterling had in his life, he couldn't control the silly expression his face made in death.

I need to call the authorities, but instead I stare at my deceased husband with amazement. He's dead, and yet it doesn't strike me the way it should.

Nothing about our relationship ever did. Forty-six years of marriage has come to an end, but I still have plenty of life to live.

CHAPTER 1

Madelyn

Please. Please.

I've only wanted one thing since I married my husband. Everything is perfect in my life. We've moved into what anyone would consider a mansion. Despite the stereotypes of wealthy men, my husband, Leo, is nothing that anyone would expect. He's caring and empathetic. He cares about my needs and the needs of others.

I knew he was different from the other rich people I've worked for.

Any woman would consider themselves lucky to be with a man like Leo. Not just because of his money, but he's a treasure of a human being. He's perfect.

I never thought my life would be easy. If anything, I figured I'd eke out a living cleaning homes for rich families my entire life. Scrubbing their expensive tiles. Sweeping their hardwood floors. Dusting their shelves with the expensive things they own on them.

Then I worked for Leo Sterling, and everything changed.

I look down at the test stripe on the bathroom counter. Waiting for the results kills me every month. I don't know why I do this to myself. It's almost a ritual of failure now. I think I enjoy tormenting myself with negative results.

I breathe in deep and think of where I started. I think of the first time I met Leo. He seemed so awkward giving me instructions on what he would like cleaned. Leo owned a much smaller house two years ago, despite it being larger than anything I would ever live in.

I remember how cute he appeared when gave me that wry smile while apologizing for telling me what he wanted me to clean. I tried to tell him that it was okay. I was used to it, after all. Usually, the instructions I received were much worse. Barely a hello from the wealthy homeowners I typically worked for. Those rich people would barely notice me in their presence, unless I missed a spot, then of course I'd hear from them.

Leo was different. He saw me. He spoke to me. He thanked me profusely after I finished. I have to admit, I took extra time to clean near his office to talk to him. He apologized when I entered and said he would move to get out of the way. I told him not to. I cleaned around him as he worked.

Not only did he greet me every time I came to his home, but he talked to me as well. It started off as small talk. I never got too personal with clients. My employer at the time warned us not to talk to the clients unless they approached you. I certainly never talked about my own life to customers, but Leo was curious.

How long had I been cleaning for? Did I have any siblings? Where are my parents from? I did my best to ignore that last question. My mother raised me on her own and she struggled financially all the time. My father passed away when I was young, and I never talk about him because of what he did. If I did, I'd worry people would have a poor impression of my family.

When I think back at our beginnings, I wonder if I told Leo sooner about my past if he would have even cared. I don't think he would have.

Over the course of a few weeks, we got to know each other well. By that time, he already knew more things about my personal life than my own friends.

It didn't happen quickly, but I soon felt tension around him. A good kind. The feelings I got in high school when a boy I liked would notice me.

It was getting harder to not say something. I didn't, though. I needed my job. I couldn't afford to lose it and the cleaning girl getting too flirty is a good way to get canned from the company I worked for. Besides, I wasn't the only maid he had. He had others come by during the week.

I wondered often about the type of conversations Leo had with the other girls who came to clean his home. One of them was my friend, Hannah. She was the entire reason why I got hired at the company to begin with, but I found myself getting jealous of her and the conversations Leo and her likely shared. She's a much prettier woman than me. I know that. Nobody would have to state the obvious.

Any man would love it if a blond bombshell like Hannah walked into their home with a duster.

I could easily imagine Leo Sterling being interested in a woman like Hannah. Who wouldn't be, after all? She had told me herself how nice Leo was. I knew that meant they talked. Despite our friendship, I didn't tell her what I felt for him. I didn't tell her how jealous I was that she got to clean his home on the days I couldn't.

But it didn't take long for me to see I didn't need to have those insecurities.

One day as I was cleaning Leo's kitchen, he walked up to me shyly. He asked me why I never asked about him. I was taken back at first, until he explained himself. He always asked questions about me, my life, my interests, but I never reciprocated.

He lowered his head and when he looked back at me, he asked me plainly. Was I not interested in getting to know him? He said he was very interested in me.

I apologized. I told him about the cleaning service rules.

Then, something magical happened. It was almost out of a romance comedy movie. He stared at me. He said nothing, and neither did I. His lips pursed as he looked at mine.

To hell with the cleaning service.

I slipped off my rubber cleaning gloves. He approached me and we kissed. The butterflies in my stomach wanted to explode out of me.

Things only became more perfect after. We began dating. Things got more serious.

And then he fired me.

No more cleaning his house. I was going to move into his home soon after. I felt like my life was a fairy tale. Cinderella found her Prince Charming.

As the saying goes. First comes love, then comes marriage, but…

I look down at the negative pregnancy test on the counter. I breathe out and pound the counter, tossing the strip in the garbage can.

Fairy tales have good endings though. I try my best to remind myself that every time I see the negative strip to not overreact. To not to get worked up.

Leo and I have been married for nearly two years now,

and it feels like I'll never be able to give him a child. I'll never have the family I dreamed of since I was a little girl.

I would joke with my mother when I was younger how I'd want five kids someday. She always laughed me off. I knew about my mother's troubles trying to get pregnant herself. I was a miracle child, she would say to me.

I walk out of the marble-floored bathroom and look at my new home. We only moved in a week ago.

The high ceilings above are adorned with antique molding and a large, dazzling chandelier that casts a soft, golden glow. In the center of the foyer stands a masterpiece – a spiral staircase, crafted from fine marble, which leads to an upper deck. Upstairs is even more breathtaking. Panoramic windows on one side face the nearby Rocky Mountains.

My kitchen has two large islands and space for a huge dining table. Currently it has Leo's older table from his last house as we wait for our new furniture to arrive. There are eight rooms on the main floor. The house itself is nearly ten thousand square feet.

We have a six-car garage. Of course, the first thing Leo did was renovate the garage to be more to his liking. He said what the owner had was dated. We've been parking our vehicles outside for now. Leo owns a black Escalade and a neon green Lamborghini. He's told me once we've settled in, he wants to take me car shopping as well.

Our home is beautiful, and I can't believe I get to live here.

I look at the barren walls. Some day, I want to fill them with pictures of children and happy family moments. I know I should consider myself lucky though.

If you were to combine the small houses down most

of my block growing up, it would maybe beat the square footage of my new home.

Leo doesn't get as upset as I do with every month that I'm without child. We have options, he tells me. If I can't get pregnant, we can use them. The people who say money can't solve their issues don't have any. Something I learned from being with Leo is that money most certainly does.

IVF is an option. I only want to use it if we have to, though. I want to do everything more naturally, but with every negative test, I'm starting to realize that may not happen. It's not that I look down on other pregnancy options. I may have to use IVF someday and I will be forever grateful that I live in a time where this exists to help me get the family I want. I can't help but feel like a failure, though.

Leo tries to tell me it's natural to feel that way. I can't help it. The failed test feels like it's ruined our day.

Today was such fun, too. Leo took the day off work to go furniture shopping with me. We have a lot more rooms to furnish and we conquered many of them today. He wanted to hire a designer to just get it done, but I wasn't for it. The one thing I loved working for wealthy families was seeing their decor. Taking in the beauty of the rooms and how they dressed them up.

Now I have my own mansion to do what I want with.

I have many ideas. I told Leo he didn't have to come with me if he didn't want to. Once he understood how much designing our home meant, he wanted to be there with me.

Like I said, Leo is different.

Maybe it was just my enthusiasm for decorating but he was just as happy as me today as we went to several furniture stores. He didn't even flinch when it came time to pay.

The numbers on the receipt would be enough to haunt me at night, but Leo paid it with one swipe of his credit card without a second thought. I hate to think of how many homes I'd have to clean to pay for just one of the pieces of furniture we ordered today.

Leo enters the front door looking serious, his cell phone held tightly to his ear. For a change he's not wearing a suit and tie but jeans and a shirt. He doesn't have to wear fancy clothes to look handsome.

"Hey," I whisper to him.

He gives me a thin smile. "Sorry," he says. "I know I said I wouldn't work today but Charles called. I had to take it. You understand, right?"

I nod reluctantly. Charles Rayer is my husband's business partner. Together they built Sterling and Rayer, a property asset company. Not a very unique name for a business, but together they manage a portfolio of properties in Calgary, Alberta and have big plans to expand their investments. I knew from the very beginning after getting to know Leo that I would not only be sharing my life with him but with Charles too.

If he's not with me, he's with him. Best friends turned business partners.

Leo walks past me into the empty living room, continuing to nod to whatever Charles is saying on the other end.

I want to tell Leo about the negative test. I just want his comfort in the moment. I need him to remind me that everything will be okay.

I get too worked up trying to get pregnant. I just want the perfect family to match my perfect life.

I had nothing growing up, and now I have the opportunity to give my future children everything I could never have. The idea of it brings a tear to my eye as I wait for Leo to get off the phone.

The stress is making things worse. My period was two days late. I thought maybe this time the outcome would be different. I told myself last month that I'd talk to my doctor about my fertility concerns if this month came and nothing happened.

I take another deep breath. Leo turns to look at me from down the hall and smiles at me a moment before continuing with his conversation.

Just that smile is enough to reassure me that everything will be okay.

I hear a curse and the sound of something rattling. Hannah walks down the large spiral staircase with two small boxes in her hand. She smiles and looks at me. I can already tell what she's thinking since I was in her shoes not too long ago.

Thank god I didn't break anything down the stairs or my employer would have got upset.

In this case, that won't happen since I'm her employer.

"Watch yourself," I say.

Hannah laughs. "I thought I was going down the rest of these stairs for sure."

"I nearly did that my second night here."

When Hannah gets to the bottom, I take the second box from her. We walk together into the kitchen. I open one of the boxes and start taking things out.

"You don't have to help," Hannah says. "I can do this."

"No way. I don't want to be one of those people," I joke. Hannah and I used to laugh about the rich people we worked for and how stuck up and snooty they could be at times.

Hannah opens a different box. "I'm just so happy that you gave me this job. Really, thanks. It was hard to get full time at the cleaning service."

I wave her off. "Of course. We need help, especially with unpacking. I just…"

"What?" Hannah asks.

"I don't want this—" I wave at the house, "—to come between us. I don't want our friendship to change. Promise me it won't."

Hannah lets out a sigh. "Well, if I don't promise that, will you fire me?" she says playfully.

I shake my head. "Not funny, and no, I won't."

The truth is I could never. I could find out Hannah had burglarized the safe in my husband's office and still not. She's been like a sister the years I worked for the cleaning service.

I was sad when we grew distant after I married Leo. I blamed myself for that. I should have done more to stay connected to her. When we moved here and Leo said we would need to hire a maid and gardener, I told him I knew who we needed.

Leo was concerned about hiring a friend though. I knew Hannah needed the money. Leo's paying her directly instead of a cleaning service too. That company gave us pennies off every dollar they made from their wealthy clients. Now Hannah gets all of that money herself.

She deserves it.

"If I ever become like one of our old clients, tell me," I say. "I mean it. It will be a nightmare for me if I ever do."

Hannah laughs. "Well, give me your nightmare any

time." She looks around the large room. "You didn't tell me how furniture shopping went."

I don't want to tell her everything. It's a stupid thought since she'll eventually see all the beautiful pieces herself, but telling her about it feels like showing off.

"It was great," I say, keeping my answer short on purpose. "The movers are bringing everything in next week."

Hannah takes out a large kitchen knife from a box when the loud ring of the kitchen phone startles me. I look at it a moment and Hannah puts down the knife in her hand. "I can get it," she says.

I wave her off. "No, that's okay. Thanks." I smile at her as I pick up the receiver. "Hello, Sterling residence." I cringe when I answer the phone. That was how I used to greet callers when I worked for others. This is my house, though. I need to get used to my own lifestyle now. "This is Madelyn."

"Is my son available?" the voice asks curtly.

She needs no introduction. The snooty tone which always has a hint of condescension, entitlement and dismissiveness, belongs to none other than my mother-in-law, Delores. As per her usual fashion, she doesn't acknowledge my existence. Not a hi to her daughter-in-law or any small talk whatsoever.

Just, put my son on the phone.

"Hey, Delores," I say, trying my best to be cheerful. "Leo is just on the phone. I'll tell him you called."

"That will not do," she says curtly. "I need to speak to my son now."

"Oh no, is everything okay?" I ask.

"My son," she repeats. I roll my eyes in response. Hannah looks at me, confused, but I nod to let her know

I'm okay.

I walk back into the foyer and see Leo pacing, still on the phone himself. "Hun," I call out to him. I step closer and get his attention. "It's your mom."

He looks at me for a moment. "I'll call her right back, okay?"

I nod and put the phone back to my ear. "I'm sorry, Delores, Leo isn't available."

I hear her scoff on the other end. "Tell my son his father is dead." She ends the call and the sound of the disconnected line beeps in my ear. I look up at my husband, and it must be apparent that things are not well, because his expression changes as well.

CHAPTER 2

"I'm so sorry," was the phrase of the day. Not only for my husband but myself as well.

Leonard Sterling senior's funeral was an event that attracted the media and the most elite of the wealthy from both this country and America. Businessmen and women with powerful last names traveled to be here.

Then there's my husband. Leo was named after his father but is nothing like him. Leonard senior had a permanent sneer on his face as if he was always unsatisfied. Leo has a permanent smile.

Due to his self-inflicted wound, Leonard Sterling has a closed coffin, but somehow I imagine that even in death he likely has a scowl in his face. I never really cared for the man. Leo has told me stories of how his father treated him, and through those, I have only disdain for his father.

Despite their relationship, Leo has been an emotional mess the past few days. It's natural of course during the grieving process, but I was still surprised by how upset Leo was. Perhaps it was due to his father's death being suicide. Leo may feel guilty on some level for not being more involved with his father.

That wasn't completely by choice though. Leonard Sterling was not an easy man to get along with. Leo is always outgoing and easy to talk to, but today is different.

He's burying his father. A man with whom he had a complicated relationship, one worse than love-hate. He craved his father's attention and, when he ultimately didn't receive it, was more upset over it.

When his father was alive, we talked about the day he would ultimately pass. When their relationship was at its lowest, Leo would joke that he wished his father would die soon. He would rather see him buried than live a life with a father who couldn't care to know him.

The look on my husband's face today makes me realize that this isn't the case. He has all the normal reactions one would expect at a funeral.

Tears. Trying his best to keep it together.

My mother-in-law is different.

As we stand around the casket as it's lowered into the ground, Delores lights another cigarette. She blows a thick blanket of smoke as the priest says a prayer.

Leo stands beside me, a hand to his face, trying his best to not outright break down in front of the crowd. He has one of the few wet faces. I wiped a few tears from my own today, but they were only in support of my husband and the complicated day of emotions he's having.

For everyone else, Leonard Sterling Senior was just a business partner. They might miss his expertise. His savvy. His influence and power. None of them miss the man himself. Even Delores seems distracted.

When the casket is finally lowered to his final resting place, the priest looks up from his bible. "And now, close friends and family are invited to the hall for drinks and dining."

The people surrounding us begin moving towards the nearby building. Leo stands over the hole and looks down at the casket. Not knowing what to say to him, I stand beside him and hold his hand tightly.

He squeezes back and manages a smile. "It's going to be okay," he says. I'm not sure why he says it. Nobody told him otherwise, but he must feel everything around him is crumbling and needs that reassurance.

"It will be," I say, managing a thin smile back.

Delores stands on the other side of Leo and holds his side. "Well, what a day, darling." She blows out smoke and I cough. Delores grabs her son's other hand, removing mine from his. "He loved you, son."

Leo scoffs. "He had a way of showing it."

Delores fully embraces him. "He did. He was a complicated man. We should get to the hall before the guests wonder where we are."

"Who cares about them?" Leo says. "They don't care about us." He nods down at his father. "Not about him either. It's all just a show, isn't it?"

"It's expected of us, son," Delores says, blowing out more smoke. "Let's just get through the day, and everything will be okay."

As we turn, Charles Rayer is behind us, his hands in his pockets. My husband's business partner looks awkward. He's always a timid, soft-spoken man, but in the moment, he seems like a turtle that wants to escape by popping his head in his shell.

"Leo," he says, hugging his friend. Instead of saying the phrase of the day, "I'm sorry for your loss", or offering apologies and condolences, Charles lowers his head. "I know what it's like."

Leo nods. "Your parents."

Delores grabs Charles hand. "I'm so sorry, dear. Your mother was such a beautiful woman. Such a terrible accident took them both away from you."

Charles smiles. "Losing a parent is hard. If you need to talk, Leo, I'm here."

The two business partners embrace before Charles walks on his own towards the hall.

Delores, Leo and I eventually make our way there too. At the hall, rich guests dine on appetizers brought out by waiters. Guests order drinks at the bar. There are enough people here to fill a wedding hall.

Delores leaves her son's side to mingle with some of the elite crowd. "Hey, darling," she says to another woman. She kisses both sides of her face as they continue talking.

"I need a drink," Leo says, eying the bar. "Would you like something?"

I shake my head. I look out in the crowd. I recognize some of the faces. Businessmen whose faces I've seen on the news and even some Canadian-born celebrities. Finally, my eye catches a man in a tan suit, leaning against the wall. He too is staring at the faces in the room. His eyes meet mine. He nods and smiles at me and walks into the crowd.

A man wearing thick-framed glasses comes up to Leo and me, grabbing my husband's arm. "Hey, Leo. How are you holding up?"

"Hey," he says back, shaking his hand. "Mr. Belrod, meet my wife, Madelyn." I smile and shake his hand. "This is Larry Belrod," Leo tells me. "One of my father's lawyers."

Mr. Belrod takes a deep breath. "I know this is hardly the time to talk about such matters, but you know how your father was. He had his ways of doing things. The instructions of his will were clear. I need to share it with you now, and your mother."

CHAPTER 3

I sit at a table by myself in the foyer of the cemetery hall, alone. I'm surrounded by the highest social elite in Canada but don't bother mingling with them. Without my husband beside me, I'm not sure they even know who I am. I recognize a few familiar faces. I've cleaned several of their homes. Not that they would remember.

At the moment, I feel no more important than I did then. With my husband not around, nobody has greeted me. They're too busy fraternizing with each other.

I'm not one of them.

It's something I knew from the beginning. Delores has done a great job at making sure I'm subtly reminded of that. One time she greeted another wealthy family, and when she introduced me to them, she reminded them I used to clean homes and that she assumed I had cleaned theirs.

I hadn't though. I'm pretty sure she said it just to remind me of where I started. Cleaning her son's toilets. Now I have his ring snug around my finger.

Suddenly amongst the crowd, as if she heard me, I spot her. Delores Sterling. Her husband committed suicide just a week ago, but you wouldn't know it the way she's schmoozing with her like-minded peers.

I look around the room but don't spot Leo. I knew

this would happen today. I understood that as the son of the person who passed away that he would have more responsibilities. He would have to be more like his mother, going about and talking to others. Delores does it perfectly.

I don't see Leo as I anxiously look round. Instead, I see Delores, still whimsically floating from one wealthy person to the next, making small talk.

Delores notices me watching her. She gives a sly smile and nods at me. I put on a smile and wave awkwardly. Part of me wonders if that's her cue for me to come to her. After all, she's talking to an older couple, likely a pair who own a huge house of their own. Perhaps Delores is again under the assumption that I cleaned it as well.

Leo had the right idea. I need a drink. I look over at the near-empty bar and spot someone else who doesn't seem to belong amongst the group.

Cero Rivera. Our gardener. Well, we hired him because he was also my father-in-law's gardener and Leo always admired his father's landscaping. I expected to see many faces at the funeral today, but not "the help," as Delores would put it.

Cero is a younger man in his twenties with a physique many would notice. Even today his bicep is revealing itself as he takes the shot glass and brings it to his lips, drinking it quickly.

Shots at a funeral? Cero is the only one doing that, but maybe he has the right idea. I could use the same right now.

I haven't spoken much to Cero. Not because he's the landscaper. He has a wandering eye, my mother would call it. He seems to notice women around him and I've caught him looking at me several times. It's made me more uneasy and less wanting to get to know him. I've thought about telling Leo about it but haven't.

He's never committed anything worse than a longer-than-needed gaze. When I cleaned the homes of wealthy men and women, I too noticed their lifestyle, and how different it was from my own, and likely gazed at them from time to time.

Hannah suddenly joins him at the bar. The two talk and smile at each other. He motions for the bartender, and suddenly two more shots are arranged in front of them.

I look over my shoulder and see Delores has noticed the pair at the bar as well. I can already tell what she's thinking.

What are they doing here? Why are they drinking at the bar? They don't belong here.

I walk up to the bar, and Hannah smiles at me. "Hey."

"Mrs. Sterling," Cero says with his Spanish accent. He wipes his face with his large fist. "Tequila?"

I make a sour face and shake my head. "No, thanks. Hannah, can we chat for a moment?"

Hannah's expression quickly changes from friendly to concerned as she follows me away from the bar. Cero watches us as we do, giving me another one of his gazes.

"What are you doing here?" I ask. I find my own tone to be a little harsh. Although it's probably better that I ask her instead of a woman like Delores. I can imagine her tone. "Sorry, that came off bad."

"No," she agrees. "I wasn't expecting to come today. I was at the house and Cero and I started chatting. He seemed emotional. I mean, it makes sense. He said he worked at his house for nearly five years. He said he wanted to come. It wasn't my idea to start drinking, though, I swear."

"That's okay," I say. "I'm not even sure this group notices us, to be honest." Except Delores, of course. I quickly turn my head and she's staring right at me. It's as if I can feel her gaze. It makes me much more uncomfortable than the one Cero gives.

"I mean, who has an open bar at a funeral?" Hannah asks.

Good question. I was just as surprised. When my father passed away, my mother could barely afford the wooden casket he was buried in.

"They served a three-course meal too," I say.

Hannah scoffs. "I'll be lucky if I can afford my body to be cremated into a jar when I die." I laugh but Hannah's expression changes quickly again. "It's okay, though. I'll ask Cero to drive us back to your house." She looks over at him as he finishes another shot. "Or maybe I'll drive." She glances around the room. "I'm more than a little uncomfortable being here myself."

I have a sick feeling in my gut that I made her feel that way. "I didn't mean to make you feel uncomfortable." Before I can say another word, Leo comes up to me.

"Let's leave," he says in a hushed voice. He takes a moment to look at Hannah but doesn't say anything to her. A loud clunk at the bar catches all of our attention as Cero finishes another shot.

"I'll get him to leave," Hannah says to me.

Leo grabs my arm with a slight grip. "I can't stay here. Let's just go, okay?"

"Of course," I say and squeeze my husband's hand. I look at Hannah a moment before Leo guides me to the exit. As we pass by the well-dressed people in the crowd, Delores is near the exit. It's as if she is guarding it against her son leaving.

Delores steps away from the couple she's chatting with to greet him. "Dear, is everything okay?"

"Yes," he says curtly. "Madelyn isn't feeling well, though, so I'm taking her home."

Delores looks at me and back at her son. "Well, it's your father's funeral. What will people think?"

"Not now, Mother," he says, looking at the floor for a moment. "Now, I'll come by later, okay? We have to go."

Leo begins to walk past her, and Delores grabs my hand. "Feel better, love." I nod back.

We walk together into the parking lot in silence. Once in his car, the conversation doesn't get better. He's quiet. His father was buried today. It's expected that he will be off, but this is something else.

I know it was the meeting with his father's lawyer. Whatever they talked about in the small room at the back of the hall upset him. He hasn't said why, and I can't help myself and try to pry a little.

"What did your father's lawyer want?" I ask.

"To go over his will. Apparently, my dad arranged it so that the lawyer would get it out of the way as quickly as possible at the funeral." He takes a moment to look at me quickly before his eyes go back to the road. "He must have planned it this way knowing what he was going to do to himself."

Leo wasn't expecting to even be in his father's will whatsoever. I don't understand why he would be upset. His father leaving him money should be a good thing, especially for Leo.

"Everything's going to be okay," he says, patting my leg.

I nod, but I'm even more confused. What did that

mean? Was something not okay? What did the lawyer tell him in that room? Delores came out of it her usual beaming self, but not my husband.

"Well," I say, stumbling over my words, "are you…"

"I don't want to talk about it," Leo says, clearing his throat as he drives.

CHAPTER 4

The tension around my husband continues days after the funeral. It goes beyond more than just grieving for his father, but he won't tell me what's wrong. He's been distant, spending all his time with Charles and avoiding home like the plague. Our beautiful new house is filled only by me and Hannah.

The upside of the past week is I've got to spend more time with my friend. I was worried about how I talked to her at the funeral. I came off too much like an employer. The past few days have helped alleviate my concerns.

I haven't laughed as hard in a long time. Now that I'm married, I still love juicy gossip about others' love lives. Hannah especially. She always has something going even if it's not steady.

We unpack a box together in the living room. Hannah places a book on a shelf beside her and reads the title. "*The Art of War*?"

"It's Leo's. He's big into mindset and productivity books." I look up at her. "So, the guy you went on a few dates with, you never told me who he was. Was it an old customer?" I laugh.

Hannah scoffs. "I wish. I hope to get a house like this someday. I just need to bag a rich dude like you. Things with that guy ended before they ever got started. It's not even worth going into."

I give a thin smile back. "Well, someday Leo and I will have to do a double date with you if you ever keep them around long enough."

Hannah nods. Before we can say another word, Cero the landscaper walks by the large window. He peers inside at us before lugging the weedwhacker on his back across the lawn.

I smile. "Let me guess. Was it Cero? That would be scandalous."

Hannah rolls her eyes. "Definitely not. The man can't remove his eyes from my ass anytime I walk by him. I'm surprised he didn't gawk at me longer just now. He did ask me out, though."

I raise my eyebrows. "Hannah? Saying no to a free dinner?" She looks at me, annoyed. "What I mean is, he seems okay."

"I guess. I don't like the way he looks at me though. Something about it bothers me. It's like I'm just a piece of meat for him to dig into. I've seen him stare at you the same. There's something about him that just creeps me out. Well, how's Leo doing? Things must be tough."

I nod. "They are, but he's not opening up to me about it. I wish he would."

"Everybody grieves in different ways," Hannah says, placing another book on the shelf. "Me, if it was one of my parents, I'd probably be less shy with a guy like Cero and have him help me alleviate my suffering."

I throw a bookmark that I found in the box towards her. "Dog. You would."

She laughs. "Sometimes people serve their purpose. Sometimes you just need… well."

"Okay, okay." I stand up and pat off some dust from

my pants. "I just wish Leo could let me support him. I try to get him to open up, but he doesn't. He hasn't been around as much either."

"I noticed."

My cell rings and I take it out of my jeans and answer it. "Hello?'"

"Any news?" the voice on the other end asks.

I sigh and look at Hannah. "It's my mom."

Hannah puts a hand to her mouth. "Hey, Angela!"

"Is that Hannah?" Mom asks.

"Yes, she's helping me unpack." I wave at Hannah as I walk into a separate room.

Mom repeats her initial question. "So, any news?"

I hate it when she asks this. I've grown accustomed to telling my mom everything about my journey to get pregnant. It was nice at first to have her support, but I'm starting to regret it. I haven't given her an update since the negative test the week before the funeral.

"Nothing new, Mom."

"Sorry," she says, knowing what that means. "Well—"

"Always next month, yes, I know."

"Sorry, I know that Leo isn't exactly thinking about that right now anyway. How's he doing?"

"Okay," I lie. It's not exactly one. I just don't want to get into it right now. "How's things, Mom?"

"It's okay. I'm looking forward to when I can visit."

I smile. "Well, all of our furniture is coming in a few days. The guest bedroom will be ready for you to stay. Leo said you can stay a few days. He says we can get you a plane ticket here too."

She sighs. "Such a hassle though."

Mom had a terrible accident a few years ago, and ever since, she gets nervous driving on the highway. Even though she lives a few hours away in Edmonton, she prefers not to drive to see us. I understand. After her back surgery, driving for long periods hurts too much. It's usually easier for me to visit her.

"I would love to see you and Leo, though," she says enthusiastically. "Is Hannah just visiting?"

"Well, no, we hired her to be our house cleaner."

My mom usually has a peppy tone, but this quickly changes. "Really?"

"Why, what's wrong?"

"I mean, she's your friend. Doesn't that feel weird?"

I look into the other room where Hannah is moving another box to the shelf and opening it. "No, it's fine. Not weird. We're having a good time."

"Okay. I guess you know. It feels icky to me, but if it doesn't to you or her, then that's great."

I sigh. A knock at the front door startles me. "Hey, Mom, I got to go. I'll call you soon. I want to come by for a visit soon too, okay?"

"Okay, hun. Love you."

"Love you too." I end the call and the person at the front door knocks again, harder.

I open it, and Delores stares blankly at me. A thick white puff of smoke escapes her lips as she dangles her cigarette in her hand.

"Oh, hey, Delores. Morning. Leo isn't home right now. You can come in, though."

She laughs, bits of smoke escaping her lips and finally through her nostrils. "Hello, dear," she says. "Leo told me he wouldn't be home, but that's okay. You can help me."

"Help you?" I say, confused. Behind her I see Cero dragging a large suitcase from the trunk of Delores's red Rolls-Royce. I was so shocked seeing my mother-in-law

I didn't notice him at first, or the multiple bags in the trunk.

She puts the cigarette to her mouth, inhales and blows out the smoke through her nostrils. "Which room should the young man bring my things to?"

CHAPTER 5

I watch as Cero struggles down the hall with a heavy suitcase. I directed him to place the bags in the spare bedroom, or at least the future spare bedroom; there's no bed in there yet.

That doesn't stop Cero from placing the multiple bags of my mother-in-law in the empty room.

I'm entirely confused, and Leo, of course, isn't answering his phone.

He never disclosed to me that his mom would be stopping by for a visit with what feels like tons of bags with her.

Delores told me that Leo offered her to stay at our home while hers is in the process of being sold. I'm sure that I couldn't hide my initial disgust. Delores laughed it off, saying that's just like her son to not share important details.

Now she stands in my living room, puffing on a cigarette, stinking up my house with her aura.

I watch her as she looks at one of the books on the bookshelf. Her white gloved hand reaches out to it. *The 48 Laws of Power*. She smiles and blows smoke on the cover and places it back.

I can feel my blood rising and wouldn't have to check my pulse to know that my heart's beating fast. How could

Leo not tell me that he said his mother could live with us? That's something you tend to share with your partner.

Cero leaves the guest bedroom down the hall. I watch him as he takes another bag out of the Rolls-Royce. Just how many did Delores bring with her? How long is she staying? Why didn't Leo bother to tell me any of this?

It's because it's not truly my home, I hear a voice inside me say. I didn't do anything to justify buying this house. It's all Leo's money. He can do what he wants. I should be grateful to even live in a house like this, compared to what I had growing up.

I hate that part of me. The voice that continually tells me I'm not good enough. I don't deserve what I have. I don't deserve Leo, or this beautiful home.

Just because I married a wealthy man doesn't mean I should act like this isn't my house. This is my life now.

Leo should have told me though about his mother. We're married. We're supposed to be a team. We're supposed to be equals, especially when it comes to what happens in our home… And this is my home.

I take my cell from my pocket and try to call Leo again, but it goes straight to voicemail this time. I let out an audible sigh.

"Any luck getting a hold of my son, darling?" I turn and see Delores. She blows out a thick blanket of smoke towards me. I attempt to waft it away from my face.

"No, I haven't," I say.

"I really don't mean to intrude," she says playfully. "My son told me to bring my things because, well, darling, I'll be honest, I'm a bit desperate. I don't mean to make things hard on you."

My face lightens. This isn't her fault. If Leo offered our home to her, then this communication issue is on him.

"Should I ask the young man to put my bags back in the car?" she asks.

I shake my head immediately. "No, of course not," I say. I do have so many questions. First off, why is she here? Why does she need a place to stay? Why is she even selling her house? When one of the richest men in Canada passes, his wife should be secure enough to continue living at her own home.

I remember how Leo was after the meeting with the lawyer after the funeral. There's a lot more going on here than I know, and it's time I get answers. Until then, I need to be a hospitable wife.

"Leo never told me you were staying with us tonight," I say honestly. She gives a bit of a giggle when I say the word *tonight*. "Besides, we don't have a bed for you to sleep in."

"The movers are bringing mine in about an hour, I've been told," Delores says, smoke coming out of her nostrils. The stench of tobacco is wafting into my face. Leo and I both don't smoke. I don't want the stench staining my new home either.

"Well, that's a relief," I say. Inside it's anything but. Now I have many more questions. Moving truck? How many things is she moving in with exactly? How long exactly did Leo say she can stay for?

I can taste her tobacco in my mouth now.

Usually, I don't say much to Delores, mostly out of fear. I always knew how she felt about me. I'm working up the courage to ask her not to smoke inside my home when I hear the sound of a black Escalade coming up the long driveway. I smile immediately when I recognize Leo.

He parks behind his mother's vehicle. After getting

out, he looks at Cero taking luggage inside our house and greets him.

"Hello, Mr. Sterling," Cero says back.

"Cero, please, call me Leo. Mr. Sterling was my father."

"No problem, Leo," he replies.

Leo walks past him and into the house. He smiles at his mother immediately and greets her with a hug. "Mom." He kisses the side of her face and Delores beams.

"Son," she says lovingly back.

Leo waves his hand through her cigarette smoke. "Are you settling in?"

Cero finally makes it inside the home with the next bag.

"Thanks to this strapping young man, I am," she says playfully.

"One last bag, Ms. Sterling," Cero says. Delores thanks him as he wheels the case down the hall.

"Excellent," Leo says. He finally recognizes me, his wife, who is also in the room. "Hey hun," he says. I don't get a kiss hello, or even a hug. I'm in shock watching what's happening. I want to shake my husband and ask him what is going on. He looks at his mother again. "And what about your bed?"

"The movers are bringing it soon, dear," Delores says. She turns to me. "I do think you need to talk to your pretty wife though. It appears you flubbed by not telling her of my arrival."

Leo looks at me with an eyebrow raised. "Oh, did she say something?"

Delores puffs out smoke. "It's not so much what she said but what she didn't say, darling." She laughs.

I looked at both of them, my mouth gaping open. I turn to my husband. "Well, it was a surprise."

He gives me a concerned look as he turns back to his mother. "Well, just know I'm happy you're here, we both are." Leo looks at me and I take his cue.

"Of course we are," I say, managing a smile.

Leo brushes a small stain on his navy suit. "I'm going to change. I finished early today."

"Wonderful, dear," his mother says.

Leo walks down the hallway and I follow him. He doesn't turn to embrace me and waits until we're in our bedroom, the door shut, before he does.

The first words out of his mouth bother me even more. "You didn't say anything bad to her, did you?"

"No, of course not," I say. "You never told me about this." I look down and see my pointer finger is directed at my husband. I immediately put it at my side. "You should have said something."

Leo nods, taking off his suit and tossing it onto the bed. "I'm sorry. Everything has been messed up. Work has been intense. Then… my father. Now Mom."

"Why aren't you talking to me?" I ask. "You could have told me about your mom. You can tell me whatever else is going on." I stand beside him and grab his hand. "We're a team. You know that, right?"

He lowers his head. "I do. I've been… overwhelmed." He looks at me, his eyes wet. I kiss him to let him know it's okay.

"Just talk to me," I say.

"Well, she's broke."

"Your mother?" I say, surprised. He nods. "But… your father didn't leave anything for her?"

He scoffs. "Barely. He went out of his way to screw her after he passed."

"Does that mean he gave it all to you?" I ask confused.

"She has to sell the house at auction," he says, changing the subject. "Even then, much of the proceeds will go towards paying the lenders back. My dad took out some very large loans near the end. He also made some large investments. And gave it all to charity."

"Leo, what did your father give you? Why won't you tell me?"

Leo lowers his head. When he raises it to look at me, a tear is going down his face. "I... It's hard to talk about."

I wipe his tears. "Try me. I'll listen. It's okay."

"Back when I first started the company with Charles, I asked Dad for some start-up cash. Initially, a hundred thousand." He looks at me. "That's a lot of money for any ordinary person. My father was far from that, though. That was a low number I thought he would instantly say yes to. Charles and I needed every penny back then – well, we still do. Despite what I thought was a low request, he refused. I asked again but this time for fifty thousand, and again he refused. I asked him why he kept refusing. I told him I was trying to make something with Charles, and when I did, he would be proud of what I accomplished. He said that he started with nothing in his pocket when he started his company. He said he wouldn't even give me ten thousand if I begged for it. Sink or swim, he told me. A man makes his own path and shouldn't ask his father to help build it for him. For a change, I talked back to him. We argued." He turns to me. "That was the first time I ever spoke back to my father. The first time I raised my voice to him. We didn't speak much to each other after that."

I hold his hand tight. "You told me things were not great with him. You never told me why." I squeeze his hand. "I'm glad you did though."

"So, after he—" He scrunches his face. "The lawyer

called me into the room with Mom. He told us the news. The majority of the money went to several charities. Mom has what little is in her savings and whatever is left after the sale of the house. We're still figuring out the life insurance, which will really help her. And Dad left me ten thousand." He breathes in deep. "The amount he said he wouldn't give me if I begged for it, he left to me in his will. Even after he's dead, he's still an asshole." He slams the nightstand with his fist and turns away from me.

I stand beside him and place my hand on his back. "I'm sorry. That was wrong of him to do."

"No... that's my father. Is it bad that I'm glad he's gone?" I don't answer him. I know it wasn't meant as a question. "Ten thousand dollars for his only son. His only child. Blind children from some charity get everything. He couldn't care less about his own child." He breathes in deep again, trying to get his composure back. He looks at me, his tears turning to rage, but his face softens when he looks at me. "Sorry," he manages. "As you can tell, I've been upset about it. I don't mean everything I say."

"I know. It's okay. I want you to be honest with me."

He lowers his head again. "My mom is broke. She has nothing. The lifestyle she had is gone forever. She doesn't seem to get that yet. I offered to let her stay here while I help her figure out what she'll do next." He looks at me again. "I should have said something to you. I'm so sorry. Is it okay if she stays here a while?"

I kiss him softly on the lips and place my hands on the side of his face. "Of course. Of course. I'm sorry if I came off poorly. Your mother needs you, and of course she can stay here until she figures it out." I kiss him again, and even from inside our room, I can hear Cero wheeling another suitcase down the hallway.

CHAPTER 6

"What?" Hannah says, her expression worth more than my mother-in-law now.

"Gave everything to charity," I repeat. "Not a dime to Delores."

"That's incredible," Hannah says, taking out a pot from a box with the word "Kitchen" written on it. "Rich people. They're truly nasty."

I nod. "This family is— was. Thankfully, Leo isn't like them. My future kids will be nothing like them either."

"And how long is your mother-in-law staying?"

I peer around the room as if Delores or Leo are with us. "It echoes since it's so empty in this house."

"Right. Sorry," Hannah whispers. "But seriously, how long is she staying?"

"Indefinitely, I suppose." The idea of it is overwhelming. "How long does it take to auction a mansion in Canada?"

Hannah scoffs. "You're asking the help? Wrong person."

I make a face. "Stop that. You're more than that. My best friend. So please don't say a word about this."

Hannah makes a gesture as if she is zipping her lips. "Not a word from me."

I breathe out. "I hope however long this takes, it flies

by. You know, at my wedding, at the church before the ceremony, she told Leo, right in front of me, that he was making a mistake marrying someone who doesn't have money. You should have seen the shock on my face."

Hannah puts a pan away. "Rich people," she says again.

"Rich people," I repeat.

"That wedding was so much fun. I don't think I'll ever have an opportunity to go to a millionaire's wedding ever again."

I hear a loud sound from outside and spot a moving truck.

"Your furniture?" Hannah asks.

I shake my head. "More of Delores's things."

"Ugh, really? How long is she staying?"

I don't answer and walk down the hall into the guest wing. I can hear Leo and his mother talking in the guest room. I'm about to interrupt them to let them know about the truck when I hear what they're saying.

"Your father loved you," Delores says to Leo.

"I know," he says calmly.

"Try being married to the man. What about me? What happens to me now?"

"I told you, Mother, you can stay here while we figure it out."

"And after here, where?"

"Maybe a luxury condo, downtown Calgary. There's Canmore too. You love the mountains. We can buy you a home there. You'll be in nature everyday. You'll love it."

"More like I'll never see you again… What of my social club, darling?"

"You told me you don't even like half of those ladies," Leo says.

"I could just stay here, dear. This house is large enough."

There's an audible pause in the conversation. I want to scream inside. If Leo tells his mother he can live with us permanently, we're going to have a lot of problems. A temporary stay is one thing, even if it's prolonged, but permanent is not something I can live with.

"We can't do that," he finally answers.

There's another pause. "It's because of her, isn't it?" she says, her voice raised. "Your darling wife, who hates me."

"She doesn't hate you, Mother," Leo says.

"You should have seen her when I knocked at the door," she says. "If eyes could kill, I'd have been murdered on your front steps. She hates me. She doesn't want me to stay here, does she?"

Leo laughs. "Mom, who truly wants to live with their mother-in-law? You didn't exactly get along with Grandma either, remember? And Madelyn doesn't hate you. I didn't tell her about you staying. It was my mistake. There was confusion."

"You'd rather your mother live on the street than take care of me, wouldn't you?" she says. "Where's my son who said he would do anything for her?"

"Stop!" Leo demands. "Enough. I've opened my house to you… *We* have opened our house to you. I want to help, but please make this easy."

"Tell me, my dear son, if you were still a bachelor, you would let me live here in this beautiful house, wouldn't you? If you didn't have Madelyn beside you, you'd let me stay. There wouldn't be talk of sending your mother to the mountains to live like some hermit."

Leo scoffs again. "Mother, Madelyn adores you,

okay?"

I'm torn. Part of me wants to enter the room and scream at my mother-in-law for the manipulative crap she's pulling on her son. It's plain as day what she's trying to do. Using me to get what she wants. Making me look like the bad guy when I've done nothing wrong.

The other side of me wants to leave and pretend I never heard a word. This is between Leo and his mother, not me. I wasn't supposed to hear a word. How would Leo have felt if he heard Hannah and me in the kitchen a few moments ago? Likely just as hurt.

I make my decision and take a step backwards, but a creak in the floor gives away my presence.

"Hello?" Leo says.

I immediately walk into the room. Leo looks slightly worried, more than likely wondering if I caught any of their conversation. Delores on the other hand beams a wicked smile at me.

"Hello, darling," she says, blowing out a thick cloud of smoke.

I smile back. "The truck is here," I say to her. "Just wanted to let you know."

"Be a dear and let them know to bring my bed set to this room," Delores says.

I look at Leo, who has an even more concerned face after my mother-in-law's request. It wasn't so much what she asked but the demeaning tone she used.

"Sure," I say plainly. I'm about to leave the room when I turn back to her. "I should mention, Delores, that this is a smoke-free home." She looks at Leo, who doesn't change his expression. "So, please be a dear—" I point toward the wall, "—and smoke outside."

I walk out of the room, wanting for the life of me to

turn so I can see the expression on my mother-in-law's face. I hope it's one of pure shock. I've barely said a word to the woman. Every time we talk, she plastered on a fake smile and talked to me as if I shouldn't share the same oxygen as her. Now I'm telling her what she can and can't do in my house.

Despite what she may think of me, this is my home. It's about time she understands that. I'm no longer the help. This is mine, and she should be grateful that we're willing to share it with her.

As I walk down the hallway, Hannah is carrying a box in her hand, about to enter a room.

"Sorry, Hannah," I call out to her. "Is there any way you can let the movers know where to bring Delores's things?"

CHAPTER 7

I hate confrontation. I've never been good at it. It eats me up inside whenever I attempt it or even think about it. My small act of confrontation against my mother-in-law bothers me. Somehow, me telling her to not smoke inside my home has consumed my mind.

Was I too much? She's going to be living with us for however much time. Was that really the best way to start this off?

She's a widow as well. She lost her husband, someone she was married to for decades, and she's had to move into her son's home to survive.

I think about what Leo told me. Her home is about to be auctioned. She has no money – well, likely enough money that a normal person like my mother would jump with joy to find out she inherited, but not exactly enough for a Sterling.

She was no longer the top of the upper class. Her socioeconomic status would be maybe high middle class at best. A drastic change for a woman like Delores.

I think about the fancy clothes she wears. The expensive Rolls-Royce she drives.

She won't be able to maintain that lifestyle now. Everything will change for her. It's sad really. Because of the actions of her husband, she lost everything.

Not only that, but it was by design. Leonard Sterling wanted to leave her with nothing. Imagine what it takes for someone to be that vindictive. He plans on killing himself but before he does, sets up his will so that his wife will be completely screwed. He gives it all to charity.

I can almost hear my husband say it. It's not about the money for him. It was about recognition. He was his only son, and instead of his will showing any evidence of that in the afterlife, his father left him his condemnation.

That condemnation was ten thousand dollars.

I could see how hurt Leo was by what his father had done.

The great Leonard Sterling. The papers wrote about his life with all of his achievements bullet pointed at the top of the article. If only they knew how cold the real Leonard Sterling truly was. The type of man who would leave his wife with nothing and his son with a vindictive inheritance. A petty man to his last moments on earth.

All of these thoughts swirl inside me as I think about how terrible I was to Delores. She moves into my home, at my husband's invitation, and I cause tension.

Sure, Delores is not an easy woman to get along with, but how would I be if I was married to a man like Leonard Sterling? Thankfully, the only thing my husband inherited from his father was his name. I'll never have to know what Delores had to go through.

I continue to unpack things and spend time with Hannah. She helps take my mind off my mother-in-law's arrival. Despite "taking a day off", Leo has been on the phone non-stop with Charles or on his cell phone or computer. He may as well be at his office.

I'm not sure if that man understands what a day off means.

After Hannah leaves for the night, I'm alone again with my thoughts. Not truly alone, though. My husband is busy with work, and I do my best to pretend that the part of the house where my mother-in-law lives does not exist.

It's easy to do in a large house like this, but I can't live this way long term. I can't let tension build further. This is my home, and if I want to be happy in it, I need peace, not this negative aura.

I walk down the hall towards her room. I can hear her talking, and for a moment I think there's someone in the room with her. As I listen, though, I hear what sounds like a whimper. The sounds are muffled by the closed door.

The floor creaks and the sound stops quickly. I knock gently.

"Delores?" I say. "Can I come in?" I hear rustling inside and steps towards the door.

Delores opens it slowly. "Yes, dear," she says calmly.

"Is it okay that we talk for a moment?"

"Of course. Is everything okay?"

I nod. "Well, it is, but I have to be honest. I feel a bit rotten. I feel like I spoke harshly to you before, and I wanted to apologize." I smile and she offers her own back.

"Well, that's nice of you," she says. "I certainly don't want this to be harder on either of us than it has to be."

"I know this is hard for you, after what happened to Leonard. I want you to know, whatever you need, Leo and I are here for you."

"I know my son will always be there for me," she says with a slight tone. "That's never the question. I may have gotten a lot wrong in life, but one thing I did do is raise that boy well."

I nod. "You sure did. He treats me well because of that,

so I guess I should thank you some more."

"Not a problem, dear. You will have to pay me back with many grandchildren, though. It's my only request."

I smile but don't say anything. I think about telling her that Leo and I are trying to get pregnant but quickly brush that thought aside. I already feel a lot of pressure trying to have a baby; I don't need Delores asking how it's going like my own mother does.

Delores takes a step forward towards me, her grin widening. "Speaking of children. You can tell me, dear." She places a hand on my stomach.

Oh my god. She thinks I'm pregnant. I take a step back. "No, I'm not pre—"

"Oh, dear," she says, her grin fading quickly. "I noticed the weight— I mean, you look different than the last time I saw you. I, well, I hoped it meant good news."

I'm not sure if I'm more angry or sad about her assumption. Maybe it's just a shock since I don't know what to say. I know I've gained a little weight the past few months. I notice it in the mirror. I'm sure Leo does as well, but he never comments on it.

"I'm so sorry, dear," she says, her grin slowly coming back. "You'll have to excuse an old lady. When the day comes, I'm sure you'll tell me when you're ready, and I'll be anxiously waiting." She grabs my hand. I want to remove it from her quickly, but I'm still in shock. "Hopefully soon, though. I remember when I was blessed with Leo. I worried it would never happen, but I became pregnant so quickly."

"Yes, I hope so too," I say, finally managing to say words. "Leo and I want children and I can't wait either. Unfortunately, I just have a food baby right now." I laugh off my anger. I suppose instead of making stupid jokes about my weight, I could get upset. I've already confronted her once today, though. I don't want to keep doing so. I just want this conversation to end so I can never think about it again.

She thought I was pregnant!

I smile at my mother-in-law. "Well, I'm going to unpack a little more before bed. Have a good night, Delores."

"Goodnight, dear," she says. I turn and walk down the hall towards my section of the house, regretting ever coming over to my mother-in-law's. I look back and see that she's watching as I leave.

CHAPTER 8

I lie in bed wondering how my life could change so quickly because of just one woman.

It was just a week ago we moved into our dream home and everything was coming together. Now, my mother-in-law has moved in, and my perfect life has a little rain cloud over it. I breathe in deep, and the sound of Leo beside me tapping away at his phone is bothering me more than it should.

I hate it when he brings his work into the bedroom. Why not go to his office? Why pretend to be tired?

I suppose I should be happy. Most husbands are likely aimlessly scrolling on their phones or looking at TikTok. My husband is making an income and doing a good job.

As if he can read my thoughts, Leo glances at me and back at his phone. "Sorry, something came up. Just talking Charles off a ledge."

"You have to do that often," I say, staring at the wall. I need my husband to talk me off a ledge right now. My mother-in-law thought I was pregnant. How freaking embarrassing is that? It could have been worse. I imagine her saying it in a room full of people instead of it being just her and me. I think about the smile on her face when I told her it was just my stomach she touched, with no baby inside.

Ugh.

"Charles always has been the anxious one," Leo says, making a few more taps on his phone and putting the cell beside him. "Me on the other hand, I like to think I can keep my head about what we're doing."

"What are you doing? I still don't understand."

"We're trying to grow capital. Making agreements with potential lenders and potential partners for equity." He yawns. "Boring stuff, but it's going to make us a lot of money. Problem is we need money too. That's what Charles is freaking out about. It's no big deal. Worse case, we take on another partner. Lose some percentage in the company. Maybe I can talk to some of my dads' friends into a loan. But that's a problem for tomorrow. How was your day?"

"This house is huge," I confirm. "I really don't know how we're going to fill it with stuff." I think about telling him about Delores but change my mind. I just want to forget about what she said.

"How has it been having Hannah work for you?" he asks.

"It's great," I say. It truly has been too. The only thing good about today was my talks with her. If I didn't have her to voice my frustrations over Delores, I don't think I could have made it through the day. I imagine telling Hannah about Delores thinking I'm pregnant. I can picture the face she'll make.

Then again, I'm already self conscious about my weight and telling someone as pretty as Hannah feels weird. I wonder what Hannah would look like with an additional fifteen pounds or so. She'd likely still be gorgeous.

"It's not weird?" he asks. "I mean, you two were

friends."

"Are friends," I correct. "I understand things change because I'm technically her customer—"

"Boss," he says.

I sigh. "Boss, right. But still, it's nice having her here. She really is doing a great job around the home. We'll be unpacked within the week, and it's mostly because of her."

"Perfect," he says, turning off the night light on the stand beside him. "What do you think of Cero?"

"The gardener?"

He nods in the dark. "I feel bad for the guy. I'm thinking of hiring him full-time as well. I mean, he worked on my father's property for years, and he did a fantastic job there. With him gone, he's out a lot of money. I think he said he has a family, too."

"He's married?" I'm shocked. The way he looks at Hannah and me, I assumed he was anything but taken. I never noticed a ring on his finger either.

"No, not married. Like, he comes from a large family. Pretty sure he said he's from Mexico originally. I think he's one of those guys that works his butt off here in Canada to send money to his family back in Mexico."

"Really?" I say. "Isn't he from Ontario, though? I thought that's what you told me before."

Leo nods. "He moved across the country some time ago. Well, our landscaping could use more work done on it. I'll hire him full-time for a few months at least. Maybe Charles could have him do some work for him after." He puts his head back. "Ah, that's right." He picks up his phone and starts tapping away at a message. No doubt I know who he's talking to.

"Was I distracting you from your time with Charles?"

I say playfully.

He lowers his hand and gives me a look. "It's just—"

"Busy. I know, I know." I sigh.

"What? What's wrong? Is today a smiley face day?" He lowers his phone at the hint of sex. Since I've become obsessed with getting pregnant, we've been using fertility strips. A smiley face result means you're most fertile. It's become an inside joke lately between us. "I didn't realize, sorry."

"No smile day," I say. "I just don't exactly want to share my bed with you *and* Charles."

He lowers his shoulder with a look of defeat. "Can you not put it that way?"

"Can you get off your phone?"

He sighs this time. "One more minute. I promise." And, as much as his phone usage bothers me, he at least stays true to his word and, after finishing his message, puts his phone down on the nightstand. He smiles at me and grabs it again, offering it to me. "Peace offer?"

I shake my head and smile. It's something he does when I get annoyed with him being on his phone in the bedroom. He allows me to keep his phone hostage until we negotiate a release the next morning, or he steals it back during the night.

"Peace offer accepted," I say playfully. I take his cell and place it on my nightstand.

"Well, what should we do now?" he asks coyly. "I know it's not exactly a smile night, but I could use a smile."

"That was extremely corny." I laugh. "But your charms are working on me."

"They always do," he says back. "I learned early on that the worse the joke, the more you love it."

"You're just one walking and breathing bad joke." I kiss his lips and roll on top of him. We continue to kiss for a few moments until they turn more lustful.

"Wait," he says, pushing me off him. "I have to message Charles."

I roll my eyes in frustration when he starts to laugh. "Not funny!" I say, striking his chest.

"That's why you love me," he says, grabbing my lower back and pushing me closer to him. His hand roams down my side and stays around my midsection. He brushes against my stomach area and his hand cups my abdomen.

I pull back instantly.

"What?" he says, confused. "I was just joking about Charles."

I cover my face in discomfort. "Your mother thought I was pregnant," I say in a whisper.

"What?"

"Your mom thought I was pregnant!" I raise my voice this time.

"No, I heard you, but why?"

"Because of my weight. She thought I was with child, instead of just being—"

"Stop it!" he says. "You're beautiful, and you know that."

I roll over to my side. Sometimes I don't know what my husband sees in me. His mother sees me as some poor, overweight woman. How can my husband think differently?

Is that what others think? I think of how slender Hannah looked in her black shirt today.

"You're beautiful," my husband repeats. "I don't understand why my mom thought you were pregnant. Maybe it was just wishful thinking."

"No, Leo. She literally grabbed a chunk of my belly and asked if there was a baby inside it." I sigh. "Like, who just assumes that?"

Leo makes a face. "I made that mistake once. Years ago, when I worked for my father, there was a young woman at work, and I noticed she looked a little larger. I asked if she was expecting. She wouldn't talk to me after that for at least a month. It's just a stupid mistake."

I turn back to my husband. "So, stupid assumptions run in your family?"

He laughs. "You know my family, right? They can all be vindictive in their ways. My mom, she's just wanting to be a grandma. I mean, she doesn't have my dad anymore. What is she going to do to fill her time now?"

"How long will she be here for?" I ask. I need an answer.

He makes a face as if trying to figure out how many days of hell I have left. "It's truly hard to say. I'm not sure. I don't want to give you an answer if I don't know. Let's just take it day by day for now."

"She won't be living here permanently, though, right?"

He nods. "You heard us today, didn't you? In her bedroom."

"The guest room," I say. "I did. I heard her trying to get you to let her stay."

"I thought so. I hoped you hadn't. Well, if you heard my mom say that, you must have heard what I told her as an answer. And what was it?"

"No," I say.

"Good. I know that my mother staying here isn't good for us, and it will be temporary. I just can't say for how long, okay?"

I nod. "I feel like she hates me."

He kisses my head. "Well, you both think the same; she thinks you hate her too. Goodnight, love." He turns over and I stare at the ceiling, taking in a deep breath. "It's only temporary," Leo mutters.

CHAPTER 9

As it turns out, despite my insecurities, both Leo and I have smiles on our faces early this morning. It's a nice way to start the day.

As he brushes his teeth, I stand behind him and hug his midsection. He spits out his toothpaste and gives me a kiss.

"Minty fresh," I joke. "Yum."

"I'm going to be out late tonight. Don't expect me home early today, okay?"

"Sure, go be with your work wife all day."

He laughs. "We joke but never, ever say stuff like that to Charles directly. The man has no sense of humor. Probably the most serious person I know."

"And anxious," I add. "You guys are yin and yang business partners."

"That's why we work out so well. It's all about balance." He pulls his tie up to his neck tighter and looks at himself.

"You're still handsome," I confirm for him. I dust off a piece of white fluff from the back of his suit.

"And you're always beautiful," he says. No matter how many nice things he says to me, I still don't feel like he means it.

"What do I do with your mom for dinner?"

"Order in. Have Hannah whip something up, maybe. She may not even be here. She's going back to her house today to get some things in order. Paperwork to be filled out. Although, while you were getting your prolonged beauty sleep after our wonderful early morning workout, I saw her in the dining area. We talked for a little bit, and she actually wanted to take you out. A girl's shopping trip she called it. She asked what I thought."

"And what did you say?" I ask, hoping, praying that he didn't give an answer for me.

"I told her to ask you." He smiles. "Peace offer. My mom is quirky, but she can be fun sometimes. Go out. Go shopping. Spend a bunch of money and go out for lunch. Isn't that what all women want?" he jokes.

"I'd prefer to just spend the day with you." I kiss him again. "This would mean a lot for you, wouldn't it?"

"Of course," he confirms. "Nobody wants their in-laws staying with them, but I hope that you two can get along. My two favourite women in my life."

"Okay. I'll go."

"Good," he says with another smile. "Now, you can go tell her that. I'm not some emissary between you two."

I sigh. "Well, if we go to the mall and she takes me to a maternity store, I'll freak out on her."

He laughs. "Can you let that go?"

"I will." I wave him off. "Eventually."

"Got to go now." He kisses me again and is about to leave the bathroom.

"Tell Charles I say hello," I say playfully.

He shakes his head. "I will, but do me a favour too. You girls play nice today." I wave at him, and he blows a kiss at me before leaving.

I get ready myself and after some time, head into the

kitchen. I spot Hannah in the dining area pouring coffee for Delores.

"Thank you, dear," my mother-in-law says to her.

"Will there be anything else, Ms. Sterling?" she asks.

"No, darling. Not right this instant, thank you."

Hannah walks past me rolling her eyes playfully at me as she does. I can imagine what she's thinking, and I have the same thoughts. How long will my mother-in-law be here for?

"Play nice," my husband asked before he left. I tell myself today will be different. I won't hold Delores to some of the things she said yesterday. I'll pretend she didn't think I was pregnant and attempt to forget about it.

If only she knew how much I wish I was. Not just to excuse the few pounds I put on recently, but because all I want in life right now is to start a family of my own.

"Morning, Delores," I say as I sit at the table with her.

"Good morning, dear," she says with a grin. She takes a sip of her coffee. She's wearing an oversized cashmere sweater with fitted dark jeans today. An orange scarf is twisted around her neckline.

"Leo mentioned you have to meet with a lawyer."

"Yes, all the things that comes with your whole life being uprooted." She smiles again.

I clear my throat, not knowing how to even respond to such a cynical comment. Smiling back or laughing hardly seems appropriate. Instead, I change the subject.

"How was your first night in the guest room?" I ask.

"My bedroom was perfect, dear, thanks for asking. I can't wait for the truck to bring more of my things, but I'll be arranging that later."

More things? Why? Shouldn't they stay in storage until she moves to her new home? How long is she planning on staying in my house?

"Wonderful," I manage to say, struggling with the words. Remember, play nice, I remind myself. "Are you doing anything else today?" I wait for her to ask me to go shopping.

"Nothing really," she answers.

"Well, I thought I heard something about a shopping trip," I say. "Leo—"

"My son always has such nice ideas," she says. "A shopping trip, just the two of us?"

This was her idea, right? Did I misunderstand Leo's words this morning?

"That would be wonderful. Which mall should we go to?" I ask.

She scoffs. "Mall? Darling, no. We don't shop there. That's for people who spend money they don't have. Put everything on credit." She laughs. "Boutiques are how we shop. Nothing has a price tag, because if it had it would likely shock you. I say that since you're not used to it yet. You will be, though."

I give a thin smile. "I've never been to a boutique before."

"I can tell, dear," she says, taking a sip of coffee.

Play nice. Play nice. Play nice. Maybe if I make these words a mantra, I will actually feel better about what I'm doing to myself.

"Oh, I didn't mean that in a rude way, dear," she says once I don't reply. "I just mean, well, you're not used to money yet. You will be, though. Being in this house. Being in the circles that you'll join soon. Leo didn't really take you to events much after the wedding. Now that you live in Summer Hills community, you'll see."

Yesterday she assumed I was pregnant. Today, she's

reminding me how poor I was. I take a deep breath. Well, technically today she's telling me I'm not a part of that world anymore. She almost wants to show me a new one, a world she lives in that many will never experience in their lifetime.

"I'd love for you to show me around Summer Hills," I say. It's true. I don't know anyone around here. Delores is likely one of the best-known members of the community.

"Of course, dear. Wouldn't be a good mother-in-law if I didn't show you around. I'm almost finished, and we can leave soon."

"I just need some coffee," I say. I'll need several to keep myself calm today. I stand up from the table.

"Why are you getting up, dear?" she asks. "This is what I mean. You don't know what you have." She turns towards the kitchen. "Oh, dear, can you bring Madelyn a cup of coffee." She turns to me. "How do you take it?"

"I can grab it," I say, embarrassed.

She waves me off and turns toward the kitchen. "Bring some sugar and cream please as well, darling." Hannah soon comes into the room and on a silver tray is a cup of coffee with a bowl of sugar cubes and silver creamer.

"Thanks, Hannah," I say. "You didn't have to."

"Not a problem, Mrs. Sterling," she says with an almost robotic tone. "Cream or sugar?"

"Uh… you can just leave the tray here, thank you."

Hannah drops the tray on the table and leaves the room. If I could see her face, I would bet money on her rolling her eyes, but this time because of me.

"Hannah," Delores says. "Pretty girl. I have to remember her name, but I do struggle with them. I used to have a bell with the girls in my old home. Ring it once and one of them would come. You only have one girl, so I'll try to remember her name. Hannah. Well, are you ready to leave?" She smiles at me and takes another sip of coffee.

CHAPTER 10

Delores offers to drive. We get into her vehicle. The inside is even more luxurious than I imagined. The interior is made of a supple leather with cherry wood finishes on the dashboard, door panels and center consol.

"How much have you ventured around your new area, darling?" she asks. "Have you seen the tennis court yet?"

"No, I haven't really left the house," I admit. "I've been so busy unpacking."

She laughs. "That's why you hired help, dear. Let Sarah deal with that."

"Hannah," I correct her.

"Right, Hannah."

I look outside the window. "We used to work together."

"When you were my son's maid, right?" she asks, emphasizing the word *maid*. There's something about her tone that bothers me when she does.

"That's right. She's great."

Delores points out the window. "There are the courts. I'll have to take you with the girls sometime. There's a prominent golf course nearby too. We like to get drinks there afterwards. I'm sure my son's a member there, but if not, I can bring you in as a guest."

For a change her tone is actually more welcoming when she says it. It's almost as if she's excited for me to be a part of her world more. "Thanks, I'd love that."

"The rec center is exclusive to people of Summer Hills as well. A beautiful pool, sauna, you can schedule a massage. Wonderful place. The girls and I go often. You'll have to come with us."

A woman walking on the sidewalk with a black tennis bag strapped over her shoulder waves at us. Delores slows her vehicle and rolls her window down. "Hello, lovely," she says.

"Delores," the older woman says. "We need to get the girls together again soon, when you're ready of course."

Delores smiles at her. "I'd love that, Lillian. May I introduce you to my daughter-in-law, Madelyn."

The woman named Lillian looks at me and waves. "Hello, dear," she says, sounding exactly like Delores. Is this how all rich women talk? In a year from now I imagine myself walking around calling everyone dear or love.

The thought makes me smile as I wave back at Lillian. "Nice to meet you," I say.

"We have to go, dear," Delores says to her friend. "Girls' shopping trip!"

Lillian waves. "See you soon."

Delores begins to drive away and turns to me. "Lovely woman." Her gleeful expression changes in an instant. "Poor thing. She had a terrible eating disorder that she's finally starting to manage. She was sickly skinny not too long ago. Like a talking skeleton." She laughs at her own joke as she continues down the road.

I nod, not sure what to say. It seems like such a personal matter to share to others about a friend.

After a few minutes, Delores glances at me again. "Have you ever tried skeet shooting?"

I raise my eyebrows. "I don't even know what that means." I laugh.

Delores joins my laughter, overpowering mine. "Well, dear, you'll have to try it with me sometime. The girls and I go often. It's like a shooting range, only outside, and you fire at clay pots. So much fun."

I nod. "Sounds great. I've never fired a gun before." I never exactly wanted to.

"You must," Delores says, and she pats my leg.

Delores continues to drive. As we do, the lots of land turn into cookie cutter large homes spaced closely to each other. Then the buildings get larger as we drive by apartment buildings and into downtown Calgary. Delores parks on the road in front of a storefront. Evalier Clothing Boutique.

"This boutique is by far the best in the city," she says. "Vanessa, the owner, is just fantastic." She lowers her head and looks around. "Poor girl is a raging alcoholic, though. The woman never found a bottle she didn't like." She laughs, waving me off. "Don't share that of course, dear. Poor girl has enough on her plate. I'm sure she doesn't want to know that her clientele all think she's a drunkard."

I give a thin smile. I wonder why all of her clientele think that. Is it because Delores has likely shared her opinion about her with the entire city?

We walk into the boutique, and I'm greeted with a faint perfume that's quite lovely. Small bronze racks are arranged against the wall with scenic paintings hung above. The walls are off-white with antique moldings, adding to the luxury of the store. Beautiful garments are proudly hung on the racks. The lighting gives a warm glow to the room.

A woman greets us with a smile and puts out her hands. "Ms. Sterling!" she cries out and gives her a hug.

"Vanessa, dear," Delores says. "So wonderful to see you. It's been too long."

"I wish you would have called ahead of time," Vanessa says. "I could have put together some outfits for you to look at. I have a few items that are new since your last visit."

"I'm not here for me today, dear," she says. Delores points to me. "This is Madelyn Sterling, my son's wife."

"Pleasure to meet you, Mrs. Sterling," she says, shaking my hand.

"Madelyn," I say to her. "Please call me Madelyn."

"Wonderful to meet you, Madelyn. Well, I'd love to help you shop today. Do you have some kind of fashion you like right now? Anything in particular that you want to try? I can order in anything you'd like."

I look around the boutique, unsure what to even say. So many designer outfits surround me. A year ago, I would have stopped and stared at the clothing, admired the materials before walking on, but now I could easily afford anything here. It's overwhelming.

"She just needs you to help today," Delores says to her with a smile. She covers half her mouth. "New money," she whispers and laughs. "The poor girl needs you to make some selections for her."

I laugh uncomfortably. It's true I don't know what to say but I'm not lost when it comes to wearing clothes. The way Delores called me a poor girl also bothers me. Is she literally poking fun at the fact that I was poor?

What does Delores say about me behind my back?

Poor Madelyn grew up in an actual poor home, the poor girl. That would probably be too tame for a woman like Delores Sterling.

Vanesa looks me up and down, a finger to her lip. "I have a few ideas of what would fit you well. Let me put together some ideas and I'll be back for you." She waves us over to a seating area. "Please, sit or shop around if you prefer."

"We'll sit," Delores answers for us. She walks over to a long antique couch. I reluctantly sit beside her.

Vanesa follows us, grabbing a bottle of champagne from a fridge. She takes out two glasses and pours. She offers one glass first to Delores then me. I thank her while Delores takes a sip.

"Shouldn't be too long," she says. "Madelyn, you look to be a small, perhaps a smaller size medium."

"Best grab mediums, dear," Delores answers for me. She looks at me and smiles. "Soon she'll be giving me grandchildren."

Vanesa smiles at me. "How lovely."

"We're trying," I correct. "No babies yet, Delores, sorry." I laugh, taking a sip from my champagne. My palate is overjoyed at the blend of crisp apple and pear.

Delores takes out a cigarette from her purse and lights it. Smoking inside buildings is illegal in Canada, a fact that Delores surely knows. Not too far away from where we're sitting there's even a no smoking sign confirming it. I wonder how much business Delores does with this boutique for Vanesa to look the other way.

Delores puffs out a plume of smoke. We sit in silence as we wait for the owner to return. A few times I think of ideas of what to say and change my mind. It's awkward enough sitting in silence but perhaps better than listening to whatever my mother-in-law has to say. Thankfully the champagne helps pass the time.

Vanesa comes back into the seating area with a large smile. "I have a few things for you in the fitting room, Madelyn. Follow me."

"Go on, dear," Delores says. "Come back and give me a fashion show when you're ready. I'd love to see. Oh, and today's shopping trip is on me, dear."

"What a lovely mother-in-law you are, Delores," the owner says. She looks at me as if wanting me to agree. I remember what Leo told me last night. Delores doesn't have the type of money she's used to living off. I know if Leo was here, he wouldn't approve, but the last thing I want to do is spit in face for her graciousness.

"Thanks," I say to her. "Truly a lovely gift."

She blows out more smoke. "Least I could do for what you and my son are doing for me. Get a few outfits, dear. Don't be shy."

I thank her again and follow Vanesa to the fitting room. I'm used to attempting to fit into small closets to try on clothes. This fitting room is large enough for someone to live in.

Clothes hang on several hooks near the mirror which takes up half the wall. One of them is a cashmere sweater, similar to the one Delores is wearing but off-white. I touch the fabric and it's beyond soft. I can only imagine what it will feel like when I put it on. Vanesa also gathered for me a beautiful gown and a dark turtleneck sweater.

As I try on each, I'm taken back by how rich I look. I try on the first outfit again just so I can see how I look once more. Maybe it's the lighting in the fitting room, but not only do I look like a million bucks but feel that way as well. I think of my mother-n-law. I suppose I almost look like her.

It's the most amazing confidence boost I've felt in a long time.

I can see why Delores loves this boutique. I didn't even say anything about what I wanted to wear, and Vanesa was spot on in the decisions she made for me. I could ask this woman to fill my entire closet, which is even larger than this room, with a whole new wardrobe for me.

I open the fitting room door and Vanesa is waiting for me. "You look beautiful," she tells me with an endearing smile. It's not a fake one this time. She can probably tell by the smile I give her that I'm happy.

"You have beautiful taste," I tell her.

"Do you need any other sizes?"

"No, this fits just right. I'll just show Delores."

"Of course," she says and waves me toward the sitting area.

When I saunter into the sitting room, Delores blows out more smoke and studies me and the outfit. I love how the turtleneck fits on me. "Darling, you look fantastic. I can show off my daughter-in-law now." She looks over at Vanesa. "Perhaps a large one in this outfit would be better."

My mouth nearly drops before I find words. "No, this is perfect," I say.

Delores smiles. "Of course, dear. It shows off your curves well."

I give a thin smile again, not sure if I should say something back to my mother-in-law. Is she trying to be mean or just making a compliment? I can never tell.

I turn to Vanesa. "I'll take the other two outfits as well. Thank you so much. I'll be coming back soon."

Vanesa smiles. "Please, call me ahead of time and I can have much more ready for you to try. Any style you want."

"I will, thank you," I say. I turn to Delores. "Again, thank you for the outfits and for showing me around."

She takes out another cigarette. "My pleasure, dear. You sure you don't want to get more?"

I think of Leo telling me how Delores's life is about to change. The boutiques, golf clubs, everything could be gone for her. Worse case, she may even have to start shopping at a mall.

"No, but thank you," I say.

I change back into my clothes and when I come out Delores has already paid for the outfits. Vanesa thanks us for coming and gives me her business card.

Delores gets into her vehicle. As I walk over to the passenger side, I look behind me and see a man. He's looking directly at me. He's leaning against the brick wall of the boutique and takes out a phone from his tan suit inner pocket.

I immediately recognize him as the same man I saw at my father-in-law's funeral. He's even wearing the exact same outfit as before. Clenched in his teeth is a toothpick.

When he notices me looking at him, he quickly turns his head but glances back.

I get into Delores's car. "I think someone is following us," I say.

"What?" Delores says, confused. "Who?"

"That man standing near the boutique in the tan suit. I saw him at the funeral too."

Delores moves the rear-view mirror, attempting to spot him. "Hmm," she says and fixes her mirror back.

"Ever seen him before?" I ask.

She turns the ignition. "Nope." She dramatically drives into the street and down the road. I look at the side mirror and watch the image of the man in the tan suit get smaller as we drive off.

CHAPTER 11

When we arrive back at home, Delores drops me off, saying she needs to take care of some legal matters. I thank her again and take my outfits out of the car. I watch as Delores leaves down our long narrow driveway. A trail of dust follows her vehicle, and the cloud of dirt overcomes Cero, who's working nearby. I can hear him cough as I walk inside and shut the front door.

I call Hannah to see if she's near, but she doesn't respond. Her car is parked outside so I know she's somewhere indoors. I walk up the spiral staircase and call out for her again, but don't hear a word. I pause a moment to take in the panoramic views of the mountains. The beauty always gives me a warm feeling, knowing I'll have this view for life.

I continue my search for Hannah. I wanted to show her the outfits I bought, but suddenly think twice about it. If I do, am I showing off in some way? Hannah's showed me her new outfits in the past. Sometimes we'd even text each other our purchases, but this feels different. These are clothes she would work months to pay for. I give up the search and head to my closet.

When I'm in my room, I have my own fashion show trying on each outfit. I take photos in the bathroom, attempting but failing to match the lighting in the fitting room at Evalier Boutique. Despite that, the outfits still look beautiful on me.

I text the pictures to my mom, and she immediately writes back.

"You look gorgeous!!!" she says.

For a change, I feel that way too. Delores may have foot-in-mouth syndrome, but I truly am thankful that she showed me around today. Maybe her being part of my life has its benefits.

"New money," she called me. It's true, I have no clue what to do with it. I've been married to Leo for over a year and never thought to upgrade my wardrobe to this level. Sure, I shopped more at Lululemon and wasn't as concerned about paying over a hundred dollars for a pair of jogging pants, but boutique shopping is a whole different experience.

I grab my phone. "Mom, when you visit, I'll have to take you to this boutique we shopped at today with my mother-in-law. You'll love it. It will be on me too." I smile as I look at myself in the mirror. The cashmere sweater I'm wearing is the most comfortable, luxurious piece of clothing I own. I think I'll even wear it around the house today.

Why not? The feeling these clothes gives me is one I want to have all the time.

My phone buzzes. I look at the message from Mom. "I'm okay. It's too much money. I don't go anywhere that fancy. So, when can I visit?"

I take a deep breath, realizing Delores is in the guest bedroom. This house is big enough with the many other rooms, and we can certainly have more than one guest room, but do I really want my mother and my mother-in-law staying at my house at the same time?

Sure, I can handle Delores and her comments when they're directed towards me. I can brush those off, but not if she says something even slightly demeaning at my mom. That would be a recipe for disaster.

"Soon, Mom," I type back. "Delores is staying with us for a little bit. After she leaves, you can come for a longer visit."

If I was expected to live with Delores indefinitely, Leo would have to be okay with me allowing my mother to come for a longer stay. My mother would be different though. She would be uncomfortable with the idea of overstaying her welcome. Meanwhile, Delores apparently has another truck of her things coming soon.

I look in the mirror at the new, expensive-looking woman staring back at me. I feel so much more confident just because of the clothes I'm wearing. I feel like I fit into the world that my husband was raised in. For once, I feel like I deserve to be in this house and all that comes with it.

I leave my bedroom and go down the hall. I see Delores's bedroom door open as I do. When I walk by, though, she's not there. Instead, I find Hannah taking clothes out of a large suitcase.

"Oh, hey," I say to her. "I thought you were Delores."

Hannah gives a thin smile. "Whoa, love your outfit."

"Right?" I say enthusiastically. I turn around to show it. "Delores actually bought it for me."

"And you thought having your mother-in-law around would be hell. Wish she was my in-law." She hangs up an expensive glittery-looking outfit in the walk-in closet.

"Have you been unpacking Delores's stuff?"

"All day," Hannah says with no expression. "I think

she's planning on staying for a while. I've unpacked winter, summer, and spring clothes. I'm working on autumn now. And yes, she organizes them by season. Before she left with you this morning, she made sure to tell me to unpack it the same way it was packed. Organized."

I sigh. "Sorry, I didn't know she was going to get you to do this."

"It's the job," Hannah says, grabbing another outfit and hanging it.

I walk around the room and notice Delores already has pictures on the hanging shelves. I don't have any of Leo and me in the house yet, but Delores already has several. I see a photo of Leo when he was a baby. Delores is proudly holding him in the picture. Leo has a blue soother in his mouth and looks calm in his mother's arms. My heart nearly melts until I notice the picture beside it.

Delores is wearing a flannel shirt with a leather vest. A large shotgun is in her hands facing downwards. She looks nearly as proud with the shotgun in her hand as she did with her son.

"You never told me that your mother-in-law was a badass," Hannah says, standing behind me.

"She told me about this firing range she goes to for skeet shooting," I say, looking at the smile on Delores's face in the picture.

"What shooting?"

"They shoot clay discs that get launched into the sky."

Hannah raises her eyes. "Well, a shotgun wielding mother-in-law. I feel slightly more concerned for you now." She laughs, and I can't help but join.

"Oh, you have to look at this too!" she says enthusiastically. She goes into the closet and comes out with a small bronze statue of two adults and a small child. I immediately recognize the man and woman. Leo's parents. The boy is Leo himself. "Someday I hope to have a statue made of me like this," Hannah jokes.

I take the statue and look at the boy. Even as a child, Leo's large smile looks nearly identical to his as an adult. I place the statue on a nightstand beside the bed. A glass picture frame of Leo and Delores is also there.

"She showed me around town a little bit today." I look back at the picture of Leo and her. On the other shelf are two more. I notice none of the pictures show her husband.

"And how was that?" Hannah asks.

"I don't know," I say honestly. "She can drive me crazy, but I also like how she showed me around. I feel almost like—"

"You're one of them," she says,

I turn my head to the side. "Well, yeah, I guess. It's hard for me to fit in. I still feel like I should be cleaning their homes and not be married to one of them." Hannah doesn't say anything, and I turn to her. "Sorry, I didn't mean anything by that."

"It's okay," she says. "I'd feel the same in your shoes."

I nod. "Then again, Delores has this way of giving you a compliment while putting you down at the same time. She talks trash about everyone behind their back. She tells me people's past history and the negative stuff. Makes me wonder what she says about me. Not to mention she called me fat."

"What?" Hannah says, confused. "She said that?"

"Not in those exact words. She literally patted my tummy and asked if I was pregnant."

"Oh, hell no," Hannah says, grabbing another outfit

and hanging it. "I would not be able to keep myself composed."

"I didn't think I was going to be able to either, but I managed. It's only temporary is what Leo keeps telling me."

"You sure about that?" Hannah jokes, hanging another outfit. She looks outside the bedroom window at the car coming towards the house. "Speak of the devil." She smiles. "Well, I should get done with the rest of the things she wants me to unpack."

I'm about to leave when I turn to her. "Listen, I'm sorry about this. I don't want anything to be awkward between us." I think of my comment just a moment ago about how I used to clean houses and realized it must have come off terribly. "I don't think of you as 'the help', okay?"

"I'm glad you said something," Hannah says. "It bothered me yesterday, but I got over it." Yesterday? What had I said to her that upset her? "I mean it was a small thing," she continues. "When you asked me to go speak to the movers about where to put Delores's things, but you were closer to the front door than me. I just felt a little demeaned."

Suddenly I remember what she's referring to. In a fit of frustration, I asked her to speak to the movers instead of doing it myself. In the moment I was upset that Delores had instructed me to do so. I felt my mother-in-law was treating me like 'the help', but then I did the same to Hannah.

"I'm sorry," I say again. "Just tell me when I overstep. You don't have to worry about being honest with me, never."

"Okay. I, again, appreciate you giving me this job."

"Still besties?" I say with a laugh.

She smirks. "Still besties," she agrees. "But only if you buy me a matching outfit like yours." She laughs. "Seriously though, I love it. How much was it?"

"Oh my," I say enthusiastically. "Nothing had price tags in this boutique."

"*Boutique,*" Hannah repeats.

"They even gave you champagne in the waiting room," I say with a smile. "It was insane."

I leave and as I walk down the hall, I can hear a hushed voice coming from the living room area. "I told you not to call this number anymore." As I peer around the corner I see Delores on her cell. She's pacing near our fireplace. "No," she says with a fierce tone. "I'm going to hang up. Don't call again. We have to wait."

CHAPTER 12

A loud knock on the door startles me and Delores too. She continues to talk to whoever she's speaking with and moves into the kitchen. Meanwhile, the person at the door knocks again, louder. The volume continues growing until I'm at the front door. I almost feel like I'm in a movie where the police are about to raid my home.

I open the door slowly. A man in a tan suit is on my porch. He looks intimidating with his sunglasses and a toothpick tight between his teeth. I nearly close the door out of fear until the man smiles, and his whole aura changes from intimating to welcoming.

"I'm sorry, ma'am, but I'm looking for your husband," he says. "Is he home?"

I keep the door held to my side, ready to close it in an instant. "No, he's not. How do you know him, sir?"

"Well, we don't know each other, ma'am," he says, with a grin. "I'm just trying to complete my investigation and need to speak to him."

"Investigation?"

"Yes, involving your father-in-law's passing." He shuffles his tie and gives me a thin smile. "Is he at his office downtown?" He repeats the address of my husband's building from memory. "Could I find him there?"

"I'm not sure," I say, confused. Why is a detective at my door asking to speak to my husband? An investigation regarding Leonard Sterling. Why? "What is this about?"

"Well, I was hoping to speak to you as well," he says.

"I saw you at my father-in-law's funeral."

"I was there, yes," he admits. "I wasn't exactly trying to hide."

"I saw you outside the boutique today as well. Why were you following us?"

"Not what you think," he says. "Can we talk? I'd like to speak with you. I need to clear this investigation from the books. It will only take a few moments of your time."

"Shouldn't I get a lawyer?" I ask.

"I don't know why you would. I'm just here to ask questions. Not here to make an arrest."

I open the door and welcome him to come inside. I wave him to the living area. He looks around at the empty room and smiles at me when there's nowhere for us to sit.

"We just moved in," I say. "The furniture is coming soon."

"Well, even though it's empty, it's a beautiful house," he says. "Hate to imagine what the insurance costs on it a year."

A bit of a weird thing to say. Home insurance was the last thing on my mind when we bought the place.

"Well, can you please tell me more about what this is about?" I ask.

"We're looking more into what happened the day Mr. Sterling passed. Leonard Sterling the 1st."

"Okay," I say. "What do you need to know?"

"Where were you the day he died?"

"Furniture shopping with Leo, my husband. That's his preferred name."

The investigator takes the toothpick out of his mouth and puts it in the front pocket of his suit, taking out a notepad and a pen. "And when do you believe you left to go out shopping and when did you come home?"

I take a moment trying to recall. "It was early when we left. Possibly nine. We came back late in the afternoon."

"And he was with you the entire time?"

"That's right," I answer. "Why are you asking these questions?"

"We're looking into some details and inaccuracies around the death of Mr. Sterling. We're just trying to understand the timelines of the people in his orbit."

I take a deep breath. "So there's suspicion it wasn't suicide?"

"Some… yes. Like I said, we just have questions and need to ask the right people to get answers."

Why would my husband be one of those people? None of this is making any sense.

"What kind of relationship did your husband have with his father?" he asks.

The question shakes me out of my spell. "Uh, well, pretty complicated."

He makes a few notes on his pad. "Why complicated?"

I remember what Leo told me last night. Of course it was about money. I feel uncomfortable telling this detective this though. I almost feel like I'm implicating my husband in something he didn't do.

"Maybe, I think it's better you speak to my husband about this," I say. "I'm not sure if—"

"Does your husband have a home office?" he says quickly, cutting me off.

"Well, yeah. It's about the only room in this house that's fully furnished." I laugh. Leo wanted to keep everything from his last house for his home office.

Before the detective can ask another question, Delores comes out from the kitchen and looks at the man and at me.

"Hello," she says, giving a smile. "May I help you?"

"Yes, ma'am, I'm Tony Cardone. I'm here to just ask a few questions."

She smirks and points a finger at him. "We've talked before, haven't we?"

He nods. "That's right, ma'am. I'm just trying to conclude my investigation."

"Investigation," Delores repeats. "Right. Well, I'd like to ask you to leave this property. If you want to ask questions, I can give you the name of my lawyer. I believe that's what I told you last time as well."

He nods again. "You did, ma'am."

"Then why are you here?" she asks coldly.

"He's a detective," I say to my mother-in-law. "He says he has questions for Leo." Tony raises his eyebrows.

Delores laughs. "Did you tell my daughter-in-law you're with law enforcement? You know that's illegal, right?"

Tony raises his hands. "I never said I was with the police or a detective." He looks at me. "I'm sorry if you had that impression." He hands me his business card. "Tony Cardone. I'm an insurance investigator, ma'am."

I look at the card, reading his name and position underneath it. "Insurance Investigator," I say out loud.

"That's right, ma'am. Like I said, I just have questions for you and your husband."

Delores pats his shoulder. "Young man, please leave

this house before I call the real police. Stop harassing me and my family. If I see you at my front door or bump into me on the street, I'll be calling your company to complain, and the police."

Tony looks at me. "Well, I believe this is your property, ma'am. Like I said, I just have a few questions."

Delores sighs and gives me a look. I glance at her and back at the investigator. "Please leave my home."

CHAPTER 13

After the insurance investigator leaves, I stay in my room nearly the entire day, only leaving to eat. Hannah picks up that something's wrong, but I don't want to talk to her. I don't want to talk to anyone.

Why is an insurance investigator looking into the suicide of my father-in-law? The answer seems obvious. The insurance company is questioning if his death was truly by his own hand.

Now there's this strange investigator man following me and asking me questions about my husband. It was Delores who found Leonard Sterling's body at their house.

How would she not be the prime suspect if anyone is under suspicion?

Sure, Leonard Sterling was a much larger man than Delores. She wouldn't have been able to overpower him. Then there was the suicide note that tied it all together.

Lying in my room, I think about what it must be like to find your husband dead in your home. I would have a heart attack right beside his body if I found Leo that way. Delores is built differently. She has barely mentioned her husband, only pointing out how his death has changed her own life. She comes off emotionless when talking about his death.

I think about the conversation I overheard Delores

having on the phone. Who was she talking to in such a hushed voice? She left the room when the investigator knocked on the door, only to reappear when I started answering questions.

Tony Cardone. That's his name. The mystery man in a tan suit who seems to be my shadow when I leave my house. I've looked at his card several times since he left. I've considered calling him just to understand why he was knocking on my front door to begin with. Why was he following me?

Or was he following Delores?

I have so many questions and no answers. All I have is my expensive new outfit.

"Does your husband have a home office?" That was the question the investigator asked before swiftly being kicked out. What kind of a question was that?

Nothing's adding up.

The idea that Leonard Sterling didn't commit suicide scares me. The fact that this investigator was asking questions about my husband scares me. The fact that Delores was the one who found her dead husband, who may have died from foul play, scares me the most.

My brain automatically jumps to the scariest idea. What if my mother-in-law killed her own husband? Now she's living under my roof. All day she'll be wandering this large house, alone with me. Not entirely alone. At least I have Hannah.

I can't calm the uneasy feeling in the pit of my stomach. What if I'm living with a murderer?

I look outside the bedroom window. The sun is beginning to set and yet Leo hasn't come home. He hasn't answered his phone either. I've tried calling him at his office as well. No answer or reply.

I think about leaving and going straight to his office. Why wouldn't he call back? The answer again is obvious. He's busy. He has a lot going on right now. It's not unlike him to come home late, but after the visit from Tony Cardone, I'm worried.

What would happen if I left home and drove straight to Leo's office? I imagine my husband dead, sitting behind his desk, much like his father would have been found.

I just want to know he's okay. I just need to talk to him.

I try my best to calm my nerves and instead read a book. Unfortunately, my love for true crime books is making it harder not to continue to jump to worst case scenarios about what's happening in my own life.

Soon I hear footsteps coming down the hallway. I worry it's Delores. After the thoughts I had about her, she's the last person I want to be alone with right now. I don't really want to speak to Hannah either.

I'm jumping to conclusions again. Why do I think my mother-in-law is the villain? I need to stop reading true crime and go back to romance. The books I've read have rotted my brain into believing the worst about other humans.

The police haven't knocked on my door. Real detectives haven't questioned me after my father-in-law's death. If foul play was considered, they would have. The only person bothering me about my father-in-law's death is some strange insurance guy who always wears the same clothes.

A knock on the bedroom door breaks my thoughts.

"You locked the door," Leo says.

"Hey!" I say, jumping out of bed. I open it and embrace him tightly.

He laughs. "I wish you would greet me like this every time I come home."

"Why didn't you call back?" I say in a harsh tone.

"Okay, maybe I don't wish you'd greet me like this every time I come home."

"I was worried," I say. "I was going to go to your office."

"Why? Did that insurance guy get to you?"

I take a step back. "How'd you know about him?"

"Mom called me," he says.

"So your mother can get a hold of you, but I can't?"

"My phone died," he says. "I got caught up with work, sorry."

"I called your office phone," I say, confused.

"Right, I'm not always there. I told you, I've got meetings all over the place. I can barely remember who and when I'm meeting with someone. I've been having meetings all day." He puts his hand on my shoulder. "You need to relax. Everything's okay. You also shouldn't talk to insurance investigators," he says with a laugh.

"Why not?" I ask. "We don't have anything to hide, right?"

"Of course not. The insurance company is trying to find ways to weasel out of the life insurance policy my father had. They're holding up the whole process of releasing the money to Mom. Talking to them complicates things. I've got lawyers on it. Just don't worry."

"You didn't tell me about this," I say,

"Well, it's not a big deal. Insurance companies are, by nature, criminals themselves. They're trying to avoid paying what my mom's owed. So do everyone a favor and don't talk to them. In fact, the general rule of thumb, never talk to anyone. Police, insurance companies. If it has legal consequences, don't get involved. Tell them to talk to your lawyer."

"I don't have one."

"That's just a phone call away," he says confidently. "Look, it's not about withholding information. It's all optics. Police, insurance companies, they have their agendas, their ideas, and want to corroborate them to confirm what they think. Having a lawyer there helps to ensure we can say the truth without implicating us into their narrative. So never answer questions without representation. That's why rich people rarely get in trouble." He laughs.

"The investigator thinks your dad didn't kill himself. He asked me questions about you and where you were, what type of relationship you had with him. He even asked if you have a home office."

"A home office," my husband asks, just as confused as I was by the question. "Listen, none of that matters. They have their ideas, trying their best to screw my mom out of what they owe her."

"I always thought that if someone kills themselves, you wouldn't be able to collect life insurance."

Leo shakes his head. "That's just the movies. Most insurance contracts have a two-year clause. If you—" he pretends to slice his neck, "—after two years, the insurance companies can't keep the money. It was the first thing I had my lawyer look into after Dad killed himself." After he says the words, he pauses. "This whole thing is weird. I never thought I'd have to call lawyers to check into these things. I want this investigation to end."

"I want this Tony Cardone guy to stop bothering me," I say.

"If he comes around again, let me know right away. I'll make sure he doesn't bother you or my mom. She told me when you guys were out, she saw him near the boutique."

"He was there, following us, or your mom. I don't know."

"It's scary," Leo agrees. "I'll make sure he doesn't do that again. Okay?" He kisses my forehead. "By the way, how was shopping with my mom?"

"Well, I got this outfit," I say. "Like it?"

"Love it! Now, take it off immediately." He gives me a lustful stare.

I smile at him. "Leo…" I say playfully.

"Come on," he says. "After so long trying to conceive with you, I know when you're fertile. I can smell it like an animal."

I laugh. "No, you can't! That's just disgusting."

"I bet if you took a fertility test, we'd get a smiley face." He takes off his suit and starts unbuttoning his white shirt. "Now, off with the fancy clothes… please. I still have more work to do tonight."

I laugh. "Having me is work?"

"Am I not being romantic enough?" he asks. "Sorry, I'm tired and just want to be with my wife. Can you blame me?"

I lean into his torso and kiss him softly. "No, I can't. Now, take your clothes off first."

CHAPTER 14

This morning, Leo left even earlier than usual. I worried what it would be like after he went to work, but the terrible thoughts I had last night don't seem so scary now that the sun is up and it's a beautiful summer day. I thought about going for a hike on a trail nearby, but I'm determined to get myself a new book.

I will definitely stay true to one of the decisions I made last night. I need something less scary that won't keep me up all night thinking the worst of the people living in my home. I'm not sure what my fascination is with dark stories but sometimes they feel a little too true.

Time for a break. I'll revisit the dark when I feel more comfortable with the anxiety of my daily life.

Until then, hunky half naked men on covers with a beach background sound fun to me. I can only imagine the comments Leo will give me when he spots me reading it at night. He's always reading some kind of self-help book to better himself. He's obsessed, really. I'm obsessed with scary things that happen to real people.

Let's not psychoanalyse that part.

I look out the bedroom window at the sun rising and it's already a beautiful morning. Off in the distance, I see Cero standing by a trail near some bushes, only he's not alone. Hannah is with him. The two are talking, very closely.

When I asked her what she thought of our gardener, she didn't have too many positive things to say. Something must have changed on that front. Perhaps the two are getting closer.

I'll have to bug her for details.

I walk into the kitchen and start a pot of coffee. I yawn and spread my hands out when the sound of a metal *ting* scares me. I look behind me and Charles Rayer is staring at me, just as startled. He quickly grabs the box he hit before it falls off the counter.

"Sorry," he says. "Your doorbell isn't working. I knocked a few times, but nobody came and the door was unlocked."

I cover my chest, trying to catch my breath. "You scared the crap out of me, Charles." I take a moment before saying another word. "Well, Leo has already left for work. He wasn't at the office?"

Charles shakes his head. "No, we had a breakfast meeting. I figured I'd catch him at home. He didn't pick up or call me back either. We really need to hire an assistant. We barely know where each other is half the time."

That makes two of us, I think. At least Leo is just as bad at getting back to his work wife as he is with his real one.

Charles smiles at me. "If he calls the house or drops by, let him know I was trying to reach him."

"No problem," I say. I try to come up with some small talk, but I always feel awkward around Charles. He looks so rigid and tense in his posture and is quiet in general.

"Thanks again, Madelyn," he says. "Have a good morning."

"You as well," I say and wave.

Before Charles leaves, Delores comes into the kitchen. "Charles!" she says enthusiastically. "How are you, my dear?"

"Hey, Ms. Sterling. I'm well. Thanks."

"The girls and I were talking about you. You're still a bachelor, right?"

Charles takes a deep breath. "Still available, yes."

"Perfect," Delores says. "I was talking with my girlfriends and we all just adore you and what you're doing with my son. I don't think the company would do anywhere near as well with just my boy running it. He needs a man like you to help." Delores grabs his hand firmly and I can almost see Charles blushing. "Well, the girls have some women they think may be a good match for a man like you. Would you meet one for a date?"

"Uh… well…" Charles tries to look away, but Delores holds his gaze.

"I mean it, Charles, you're such a catch. You should meet one of these women they want to set you up with. Plus, some of them are quite gorgeous. I'll set those dates up first."

He laughs awkwardly. "That sounds great. Thanks. Maybe not now, though. Things are very busy at the moment."

Delores finally lets go of the man's hand. "Do take care, Charles. Tell my boy I love him when you see him next."

The curse of bad small talk doesn't seem to impact my mother-in-law with Charles.

"I will," he says with a smile and waves before walking out of the kitchen and towards the front door.

"Poor thing," Delores says as she watches him. "His mother and father both died last year." She shakes her head. "Can you imagine?"

"Car accident, I think, right?"

"That's right, dear. Poor man." Delores turns to me. "Did you eat breakfast yet?"

"Uh, no. I just woke—"

"Perfect," Delores says with a smile, cutting me off. "We're going for brunch, dear. Me, you and the girls. I want you to meet them."

When it finally hits me that this isn't an invitation but a demand, I agree to go.

"Perfect, dear," she says, her smile fading for a moment.

CHAPTER 15

I sit in the passenger seat as Delores drives again. As we pass the tennis courts, she points them out to me again even though she had the day before. I nod and don't let her know that we already talked about this.

"Today, we're having brunch with the girls at the golf course. I'll use my visitor pass to get you in," she says. "They have a wonderful brunch. Nearly everything you can want, they have, even crab legs and lobster. I tend to just stick with an egg white scramble with tomatoes, but you'll love it. They have all the standard breakfast items. Bacon, potatoes and, oh the pancakes are to die for." She smiles.

I smile back. Why would I love all the fattening food? It's just as I told Hannah yesterday: Delores has a way of making a neutral statement feel like a punch in the gut with her delivery.

"You don't speak much, dear," she says to me, glancing at me a few times as she waits for my response.

I smile. "Well, my mother said I always did keep to myself a little too much."

"I hear you and my son giggling like children in your bedroom all the way down the hall. Obviously you're not shy with everyone. It isn't just me though, is it?"

"No, of course not," I lie. I wonder: if she can hear Leo

and I laughing in the bedroom, what else can she hear? I try to get that image out of my head. I think of telling her that I feel the same way around Charles Rayer but decide to keep that to myself as well. "Leo's different," I finally say.

"He's in love. I can see it when he looks at you, or the way he talks about you. You've been married for a little while now, and he's still a smitten kitten with you." She makes a clicking sound in her mouth. "That's special. Some couples never have that. They marry for other reasons." She pats my leg. "Yours is special, though. Some of that, of course, is because my boy is special. I'm starting to see what he sees in you. You're a good person."

I give a thin smile. "Thanks, Delores."

"I suppose my darling son told you about what's happening with the insurance company regarding my husband's policy?"

I look away from her. "He has, yes. I'm sorry that's happening."

"It's been a nightmare, truly. Lawyers are involved. They're trying to say that his will was direct in that the money was to go to charities. We're fighting. They're trying to take everything from me." She shakes her head.

This I wasn't aware of. Leo told me other reasons.

"That's terrible, Delores. I do hope that this gets settled soon." If only she understood how much of an understatement that is. More money in Delores's bank account means less days at my home. For a change, I hope the blind children get less money and it goes to my mother-in-law for the most selfish of reasons, mostly my sanity.

Delores opens a window and takes out a cigarette. "Hold the wheel, dear," she says and lets go without hesitation. I quickly grab the steering wheel to keep the car going straight as she lights her cigarette.

"Do you have a will, dear?" she asks, glancing at me. "Life insurance?" I don't answer. Why is she even asking me? "Dear, you really should have one. Make sure when you do the wording of your estate – well, Leo's estate I suppose – is clear. You don't want to be in my shoes."

We continue to drive in silence, her blowing smoke out the window, until she resumes again with more odd comments. "If you want, you could add me to your will. If you have children, you want to ensure they have the best life has to offer. Fingers crossed, if something terrible happens to both you and my son, who would look after your future children? I hope you know I'd take that responsibility in a heartbeat, dear. You should ensure to leave your estate to your future children in trust and money to their guardian to ensure they have everything they need to be successful." She shakes her head. "Just look at poor Charles. One moment he has two parents, the next, they're both six feet under." She looks at me. "You never know what life has in store for you." She blows smoke out the window.

CHAPTER 16

Delores drives up to the gates of Summer Hill Golf Course and smiles at the security guard as she lowers her window. "Ms. Sterling," the guard says. "Welcome back."

"Hello, dear. I have a guest with me today. My daughter-in-law."

I smile and wave at the man. He nods back. "Enjoy the brunch, you two."

Delores drives in and I take in the view of the course. Meticulously manicured grass stretches out with the nearby mountains as backdrop, adding to the beautiful scenery.

She parks in a VIP lot close to the front of the building. As I get out of her car, the smell of fresh cut grass greets me.

There are many women and men dressed in expensive clothing coming and going from the clubhouse. With my outfit, for a change I feel like I belong. I wonder what the joint net worth is of the people here.

"This way, dear," Delores says. As we walk into the building, Delores waves and smiles at a few people walking by. One of them stops and she introduces me as her daughter-in-law. For a change she seems happy to do so.

The brunch is outside. Rows of buffet trays line

the edge of the dining area. Taking a glance, I see an incredible selection of seafood, freshly squeezed breakfast drinks and deli meats and cheeses. A chef is standing at his station ready to make egg dishes on request. The food looks amazing. The aroma of freshly brewed coffee and pastries fills the air as the finely dressed patrons exchange pleasantries. Each table is adorned with folded linen and elegant fresh flower arrangements.

I'm about to pick up a plate to dig in when Delores whispers, "Not your usual buffet, darling. There's a menu at the table and the waitress assembles your plate for you." She smiles at me.

Waitresses for a buffet? What backwards world am I living in?

A small group of women sit in the center of the dining area. They laugh amongst themselves until one of them notices Delores and stands up. I remember her as the woman Delores said had an eating disorder. Lillian, I believe her name is.

"Delores, dear," she says, sounding almost exactly like my mother in-law. "How are you?"

"Very well, Lillian. Ladies, this is my daughter-in-law, Madelyn."

Each of them introduces themselves. There's six of us at the table and I forget nearly all their names immediately. All except one, Christine. Delores said that her friend group was not all ladies her age, but so far Christine is the only woman born in my decade.

She shakes my hand and offers me an empty seat beside her. "Nice to meet you," Christine says.

"This is Christine Mills," Delores says, introducing her again. "Her husband, Patrick Mills, owns the largest flooring company in Calgary. Lovely woman."

"Thanks," Christine says to Delores. She looks at me. "We've heard so much about you from Delores. So happy to meet you in person."

I give a thin smile. I can only imagine what my mother-in-law has said, but given Christine's genuine interest in me, maybe it wasn't quite so negative. As I continue to talk to my mother-in-law's friends, I realize they're all actually easy to talk to. This group enjoys laughing. We're the loudest table at the brunch. All of them seem to know each other well and appear to have a strong bond, with plenty of inside jokes. Besides the designer clothes they wear, I wouldn't know they were some of the wealthiest women in Calgary.

All of them appear to adore Delores, especially Lillian. She laughs more at what Delores says than is necessary. You can tell from how they treat my mother-in-law that she's the head of this friend group. I almost feel like I'm sitting with the cool kids at high school being with them.

We order our food and drinks. The waitresses bring them quickly.

Christine leans towards me. "Do you play tennis?"

"Not really. I would love to, though. Delores drove me by the tennis courts and rec center. I'd love to come."

"I can help you learn," Christine offers. "I used to be on a team back in high school. We all love to play together. I'm sure you'd have fun."

"I'd love that. Thanks."

I look at the food on everyone's plate. Most of it is the healthiest options available. Their plates are half empty. Compare that to mine which is filled to the brim. Some of my food is layered on top of each other even. Isn't that what you do at buffets?

The group continues to laugh as Delore's friends talk more about the community.

"Have you girls met the new girl that lives on Mountain View?" Lillian asks.

Delores nods. "Where Sandra Daunting used to live, right."

"That's the house. Well, you should see the new woman who lives there. Every time I pass by and she's outside, she's wearing some eccentric outfit full of colors. It's like she shops at a clown store or something."

The table erupts with laughter, even though the comment was quite mean. Other tables can easily hear us. I can only imagine if one of the other people know this woman what they must think. I'm taken back by how mean-spirited Lillian's comment was, until another woman makes a similar mean one. Some other woman apparently gained twenty pounds. The girls laugh again in unison about how this person's diet is not going so well. There's suspicions that another woman's husband is having an affair and for some that's hilarious as well.

I realize this group of women may not be as nice as I first thought. I'd hate to know if they were talking about me this way. Knowing Delores, I wonder if they have in the past.

As the girls continue to laugh at others' expense, I'm happy to notice that Christine doesn't join in. She appears to be the only woman at this table with some decency. Delores is at the other end of the spectrum however, dishing out as much gossip as she can.

Lillian continues to laugh the hardest in the group, but I wonder what she would think if she knew what Delores said about her behind her back.

"How did you and your husband meet?" Christine

asks.

I smile. "Well, it's a fun story," I say, worried what this group of women will think.

Delores takes a nibble of her egg whites. "She was Leo's house cleaner."

"No way!" Lillian laughs, thankfully not as loud this time, but still her chuckles are starting to bother me to my core.

I smile back at her. "Yeah. I worked for him, and he was just the nicest man. I don't usually talk to customers at their home, but he was so intrigued by me. We started talking and soon, well." I raise my finger and show the ring.

"What a wonderful story," Christine says. "Like a fairytale."

Delores laughs. "A real Cinderella, my daughter-in-law is."

"Are you from Calgary?" Christine asks me.

I take a small bit from my large plate of food. "No, from Edmonton originally."

"That must be hard for your parents, being out there."

I smile. "It can be, yeah. I'm hoping to visit my mom again soon."

"How nice." There's something about her that's very welcoming. I'm not sure if I can fit into Delores's group of friends, but I'd like to get to know Christine better. "My father just retired last week by the way," she says to the group. A few of them clap. "My mother isn't so happy now that he's home more." Lillian laughs but not as hard as she would have if Delores made the joke. Christine looks at me. "Is your father still working?"

"Well—"

Delores answers for me. "He's passed away."

Christine puts her fork down. "I'm so sorry. I didn't know."

I shake my head. "It's okay. It was a long time ago."

Delores takes another bite of her food and covers her mouth. "Her father was actually famous."

"No way?" Lillian says with a wide grin. "What did he do?"

"Rob people." Delores laughs. "He was in the paper some time ago. I have the headlines, dear. I'll have to show you."

Lillian puts a hand over her mouth, covering her smile. "Oh, well."

Delores continues to dig into my past. "Unfortunately, he passed away in prison, Leo told me." She looks at me. "Poor girl had no father growing up."

An audible *aww* comes from the group of ladies. I feel so awkward and want to leave but manage a thin smile back. "My mother raised me by herself."

"Good for her," Lillian says. "I have such respect for single mothers. They have to do so much on their own. If I didn't have my husband or nanny, it would have been unbearable to have my three children." She laughs.

I nod back but don't say a word. How could these people even function without their wealth?

Delores sighs. "I have to admit how pleasantly surprised I was at how well put together my daughter-in-law is. A father in jail, a girl raised in a rough community in Edmonton? When I found out about her past and how she grew up, I half expected her to have too many daddy issues to marry a man like Leo." The group of girls laugh. Delores smiles before she continues. "I worried my son would drag home some girl I'd have to watch to make sure didn't steal the silverware, or worse, some crackhead."

The table erupts with laughter, with Lillian the loudest of the group. My mouth drops at the comment and I lower my head, but their laughing feels like it's going on forever. Even Christine is covering her mouth, with small giggles coming out.

Finally, the laughter stops and they move on to talking shit about some other poor girl that Delores is now gossiping about. I wait a few minutes to not make it so obvious. When I stand up from the table, Delores looks at me.

"You okay, darling?" she asks with a wicked smile.

I nod. "I'm sorry, where's the bathroom here?"

Delores points inside the building. "Down the main hall near the receptionist there."

I smile as I leave the table, trying my best to maintain my cool. Part of me wants to break down and cry in front of these terrible women; the other wants to scream at each other individually, saving Delores for last. I glance at Christine. I had high hopes that I could have become friends with her until her behaviour showed her true colors.

As I leave the table, the group of women erupt with laughter again and part of me wonders if it's at my expense.

CHAPTER 17

As soon as the taxi stops in front of my gate, I let the driver know he can just drop me off. When he leaves, I put in the password and the gate opens. Once inside, I put the password in again to have it shut. I walk the long driveway to my house and head right into my bedroom and do not leave. I immediately take off my fancy clothes and put on what I would usually wear.

I can't get what those ladies did to me out of my head. Never have I felt so low. I felt so small compared to them. It's as if they summed up all the worst highlights of my life. Poor Madelyn. A father who died in jail. I must have daddy issues.

I can only imagine what Delores said about me after I left.

"Poor girl. She had nothing before she met my son. Now she thinks she's entitled to the life we have because she married him."

I hope she realizes when I don't come back from the bathroom that I left because of her antics. I was actually somewhat happy when Delores wanted to show me around more and introduce me to her friends.

Now I see it was all a ruse to embarrass me. Throw egg on my face. She wanted me to feel the sting as her and her friends made fun of me and where I came from.

I may not have had a father for most of my life, but my mother was loving, caring and would never treat another human being how Delores treated me. She's cruel, abusive, and manipulative. If she was here right now, I'd— I take a deep breath, trying to collect myself.

Then the image of her friends laughing at me strikes me. Sure, Delores said the mean things in a joking form, but it was completely at my expense. The girls laughed not because of a joke, but because they thought I was the punchline. My life.

The idea that this woman will be coming back to my home, laying her head down in my guest room, makes me sick.

She needs to leave. She has to go. I can't stand her in my house any longer.

I hear the sound of a large vehicle coming down the driveway. When I look outside, I see a moving truck. The furniture company must be coming early. I grab the notebook where I wrote down all my notes of what is going where. There's so much furniture and rooms to fill that it will be hard to remember without it. It took me a while to decide how to place everything. I even drew designs in my book of how I wanted it.

For a change, I smile, breaking my angry mood at the idea of decorating my new house, no, my mansion. This is mine. Not Delores's home. In fact, her house is going up for auction and she'll have nothing soon. It's childish of me, but the idea of that makes my smile wider.

I wonder what her judgemental friends will think of Delores when she's broke and can't pay the bill at the golf club. She won't even be able to afford a membership soon enough. I will, though.

I leave the bedroom and go down the hall. The

moving truck parks right near the entrance.

"Hey," Hannah says, standing beside me. "I haven't seen you much today. Everything okay?"

"It is now, yeah," I say as I wait for the movers to come out. "The new furniture is here."

"They're a few hours early. I was going to go to the grocery store to grab some things for dinner. Want to come?"

I look at her. "Well, I would but the movers will need me to tell them where things are going."

"No problem," Hannah says. "I'm just going to clean the kitchen before I head out."

Before she leaves, I grab her hand. "Wait, sorry." I let go of her. "I just want to say, I'm sorry. I feel like I haven't treated you right the past few days."

"It's okay," Hannah says. "I know you're stressed right now."

"No, it's not okay. The last thing I ever want to be is like—" I see Delores's Rolls-Royce drive up. "Well, her."

Hannah looks at Delores approaching and back at me. "What's wrong?"

"I'll tell you later. Do yourself a favour and leave before you have to talk to her. I wish I could, but I'm stuck with her for life."

"Or just until she moves out," Hannah reminds me.

"Which will be soon."

Hannah leaves into the kitchen as Delores comes out of her vehicle. She greets the movers. "Hey, boys," she says enthusiastically. "Bring most of the boxes to the first few rooms on the left when you enter the house. Are you able to be gentlemen and help me set up the furniture the way I'd like? There's a wonderful tip included." She smiles.

"Of course," one of the movers says with a wide smile

of his own. "We'll start unloading and move things how you want later."

"Wonderful," she says.

The movers open the back of the van to reveal mostly boxes and some furniture, including a desk and office chair. None of it is the furniture I shopped for with Leo. It suddenly dawns on me that this whole truck is full of Delores's things.

The entire truck.

There is an absurd amount of belongings inside and none of it belongs to me. It's all my mother-in-law's. And all of it is going inside my house. My mother-in-law will own more things in my home than I and Leo do combined.

What is she doing?

"Where'd you go, darling?" Delores says as she walks up the steps. "I was worried when you didn't come back to the table."

I think about yelling at her. I think about confronting her. I'm not even sure what to say in the moment. I think of Leo. The last thing he wants to hear about today is how his mother and I got into a tiff.

"I didn't feel very well," I say to her.

Delores nods. "Next time, tell me, dear, and I'll drive you home." She turns to the moving van. "It's nice that my space will feel more like home." I don't comment and instead try and hold back my rage and stop my mouth from acting out what my entire body wants to scream at her. "What's that in your hand, dear? A journal?"

I look at the notepad. "My movers are coming too today. In a few hours. There's a lot of things coming so I wrote down where it all goes and how I want the furniture to look."

"That's wonderful, dear," she says, taking out a cigarette and lighting it. Smoke comes out from her nose as she exhales. "Isn't moving into a new home grand?"

My home. This is my home. You wouldn't know it from the number of things Delores is having brought inside at the moment. "Be careful of that, young man," she says as a mover walks inside with a box. "Valuable chinaware."

"No problem, Ms. Sterling," he says.

Chinaware? She brought her plates to my house. Why? I'm not using her chinaware. I have my own. I don't want to eat off anything she owns. I don't want any of her stuff in my kitchen. I don't even want her in my home.

Delores walks inside, her cigarette loose in her hands. She blows out smoke in my foyer as she supervises the movers. Just a few nights ago, I asked her to not smoke inside either.

The woman has no boundaries, or she just doesn't care what mine are.

It's like she's a virus that's grown, duplicated itself in days, and has completely taken over half my house. Soon the entire place will belong to her.

"Delores," I say, feigning a smile of my own, "can you please smoke outside?"

"Oh, right, dear," she says as if she's confused. Instead of walking back outside, she goes to the nearest window and opens it, blowing more smoke through the mesh screen. "Can you bring that box to the second room on the left," she directs the mover. "And when you get to the desk, that will go into the third room down this hallway."

"No problem," the mover says back.

"Fantastic," she says to herself, blowing more smoke out of her nose. Most of it stays indoors and not out the window. Did I not make myself clear? I wonder. I didn't ask her to open a window and smoke. I asked her to leave my home and do it. Delores treats me the same as Vanesa from the boutique. She thinks she can do whatever she wants in my house, despite what I say. I could put a no smoking sign and nail it on her and she'll still puff away on her cancer stick.

Then I see two of the movers start to move a large desk.

"It'll be nice to have an office again," she says.

An office? Why does a woman who doesn't work need one? Why does she need an office in her temporary home that doesn't belong to her? Did she tell the mover to put it into a third room down her side of the hallway? She'll be occupying three rooms in my house? I only take up one myself.

Hannah walks past us, car keys in her hand. "I'll be back in a while," she says. "Text me if you need anything from the store."

"Thanks, Sarah," Delores says to her. Hannah doesn't respond.

"Her name is Hannah," I say, articulating each syllable in her name. "Hannah," I repeat. "And smoke outside. I didn't ask you to crack open a window."

Delores opens her mouth in disgust. "Such a tone, young woman. Why would you talk to your mother-in-law this way? Do you speak to your own mother with such an attitude? I hope, no, pray not. I—"

Out of frustration, I turn and place my notebook on the bookshelf nearby. "I'm leaving," I say to her. I quickly run after Hannah, who's getting into her vehicle.

CHAPTER 18

It doesn't take long for Hannah and me to get everything on the shopping list. What's slowing us down, however, is me telling her how miserable I've been since Delores moved into my house. Hannah can't believe how they treated me at lunch. As we leave the grocery store, I spot a McDonalds across the street.

"Are you hungry?" I ask her. "On me."

She laughs. "Didn't you just have brunch? You're still hungry?"

"Starving!" I exclaim. "You should have seen how much food they had at the golf club brunch, and yet none of it was on their plates. It's like those people don't know how to properly eat at a buffet."

"Those people. Aren't they your people now?" she says playfully.

I shake my head. "I want nothing to do with them. What I do want is a Big Mac though. Large fries!"

"Okay, you sold me." Hannah laughs.

We dine inside. Hannah asks if I needed to go back home soon for the furniture movers, but I let her know that I have a few hours before they arrive. Besides, if I see Delores directing her movers any longer, I'll have a complete meltdown.

"I still can't get over how terrible that brunch was,"

I say as I take a large bite of my burger, The taste of my economically priced meat may be much cheaper than the cuts chosen for those at the golf course, but I'll take this burger any day of the week over theirs.

"They're like a bunch of school children," Hannah says while eating a single fry. "Worse than high school. I didn't want to say anything with Delores there, but why does she need to have an entire moving truck full of her things come to your home? Has the woman never heard of a storage facility?"

"Too low class for her," I joke. "She needs to house her items in someone else's mansion… It's supposed to be temporary. I can't wait for Leo to get home, though. I need to talk to him."

"You need him to act like a big boy and tell his mother to move out." Hannah laughs.

I think of how upset Leo was, talking about how his mother will have to change her whole life. Then I remind myself what Delores is like with the lifestyle she had. She doesn't deserve it. She uses it to put other people down.

"I need her gone soon," I say, eating a fry. "I can't live like this. I tell her to smoke outside, and she cracks open a window and smokes inside my home right in front of me. Ugh! And I haven't told you the worst of it."

"What do you mean?"

I tell her about the insurance investigator, Tony Cardone, and his strange questions. I explain how Leo and Delores both told me never to talk to police or investigators.

"Always have a lawyer is their advice," I say to Hannah.

"I hope I never have to use it," she says. "This is a bit much, though. So this investigator thinks it wasn't a suicide? What does he think happened?"

"I try not to think about it. He asked a lot of questions about Leo. Asked if he had a home office for some reason." I think of the movers at my house who are setting up Delores's office as we speak.

"You think it was your mother-in-law?" Hannah asks. "Do you think she could have… you know?"

I nod. "If she had the strength, I wouldn't doubt it. She's a twig, though. Smaller than you," I say as Hannah has another fry. "Which, by the way, how do you stay so skinny?"

Hannah laughs. "Seriously, though, do you think it wasn't suicide?"

I take a moment to answer. "The police aren't knocking on my door. I've never been questioned by an actual detective." I think about Tony Cardone again. "That insurance investigator is sneaky. He really made me think he was a cop."

"So, worst case, you have a murderer living with you," Hannah says mockingly.

"She's murdering my ability to have happiness," I say playfully. "I just need her to leave soon."

"Talk to Leo," Hannah says. "He's a reasonable guy. I can't imagine him wanting his mother to live with him long term."

I nod. I think of Hannah and how I saw her having a private conversation with our gardener. "Speaking of men in our lives, I spotted you speaking with Cero this morning. Do you have anything to report?" I sip from my straw, my eyes wide, waiting for a reply.

"That man's a flirt," she admits. "A real smooth talker. I have to say, he's growing on me. Maybe at some point I'll take him up on his offer for drinks."

"So, he's already asked you out?"

She laughs. "Several times. Each time I shoot him down. I have to work at your house every day. If things don't go well, I have to see him every day. I don't like that idea."

"Fair enough," I say, finishing my burger.

"Should we go back to your house?" Hannah asks.

I shake my head. "Let's take our time. I'm enjoying myself too much to go home."

As Hannah turns into my long driveway, we drive past Cero, who's trimming a large bush. He stares into the car as we drive by.

"I think he's going to ask you out again today based on that look he just gave you," I joke.

"And going to be shot down once again." Hannah laughs. She parks near the front of the home and to my surprise a new moving truck is now parked where the old one once was.

"My movers are here," I say. "Really early too." I look at the time on Hannah's car clock.

We get out and walk inside. In the living room, Delores is instructing the movers where to place a large sectional. The entire living room is already arranged.

The truck is already nearly empty.

"Just right there, boys," Delores says, blowing out smoke in the middle of the room. The men listen and Delores takes a step back. "Perfect. Looks beautiful there."

Beautiful? No, the furniture may look nice but that's because I picked it out. How it's placed in the room is nowhere near how I wanted it to be. I look at Delores, stunned.

"The movers are nearly done," she says.

"Delores, why didn't you call me to let me know the

movers were here?" I ask.

"Well, dear, I knew you were out with your friend, Hannah," she says, smiling at her. She looks back at me. "I was hoping time away would help you cool off."

Cool off?

I hadn't even noticed the other mover on a ladder in the living room until he starts sticking a nail into the wall. He goes down the ladder and back up, hanging a large picture prominently in my living room. It's a picture of my husband and his mother.

"Love how this room looks now," Delores says with a grin. "Has a nice feng shui to it, doesn't it?"

CHAPTER 19

After my exchange with my mother-in-law, I spend most of my time with Hannah waiting for my husband to come home. I can't wait for him to come through the doors so we can talk about what's been happening.

I've had enough.

But I know I'll have to wait to tell him. He'll be coming home late, as usual. I've already texted him saying we have to chat when he gets in. Seems ominous enough. I don't want to text it all out to him. I won't call him to complain about his mother either. This has to be a conversation we have, alone and in person.

To my surprise, Leo walks through the door much earlier than expected. It's not even five in the afternoon and he's home. I can't help but smile when I see him.

"Good luck," Hannah whispers to me. I give her a nod before going to my husband.

"You're home early," I say. "Good."

"Whoa," he says, looking around. "Our house actually looks like a home now. Love how you set it up, too. Great work. Are you going to show me the rooms?"

I breathe in deep. "Not yet, not until I get it how I want it."

He looks at me, confused. Delores suddenly materializes in the room and hugs her son. "Leo, darling," she says enthusiastically. "Isn't your home wonderful?"

"Yes, Mother. And the movers came for you too?"

"They have, son. Thanks for helping me get that organized."

"Of course," he says.

I look at him, my eyes extinct of any love at the moment. How many more trucks coming to our home has my husband organized for his mother? How long must I stay in this house with her?

"Can we talk?" I ask. I glance at Delores. "In private."

Leo looks at his mother and at me. "Is everything okay?"

"Can we talk?" I repeat.

"She's upset with me again, dear," Delores says. "I don't understand why."

Leo looks at me. "Okay, well, let's go to our bedroom."

When we're inside, I peer down the hallway to ensure his mother isn't following us before closing the door.

"That was really awkward," he says. "I came home early. I got a message from both you and my mom and you are both saying you want to talk to me. I mean, I knew that meant something happened. I actually had this nice idea that I'd come home early just so the three of us could break bread together. Share a meal. Maybe with me there we could, I don't know, get rid of this tension."

His words hit me for a moment. My rage escapes me until I remember everything Delores has done since moving in. "I'm having a hard time with this, Leo," I say. Understatement of the century.

"Why?" he says. "I don't understand."

"I mean, first there's this huge truck full of her things. She had four movers moving her belongings into three of our rooms. Three! I didn't realize she was setting up her own home within our home."

"Well, I knew she had some things to bring. I didn't realize it would be that much. I said I'd organize a storage locker for her, but she said she would take care of it."

"Well, she did. Our house is her storage locker."

He lowers his head and sighs. "Okay, well it's just her things. It's not like we don't have the room or anything. This house is huge for the two of us. Her things won't stay here. If her new place can't keep all her crap in it, I'll organize a storage locker myself. Okay? This isn't a big deal."

"That's fine, but I don't understand how long she's planning on staying here. How many more trucks are coming?"

"That's it," he says. "Well, as far as I know. Look, I'll talk to her if her things in our home bothers you. I'll make sure she has a storage locker and the movers bring anything else there. This is just—"

"Temporary, yes, I know."

He takes a step back and loosens his tie. "Gosh, what has come over you? You're so tense."

"That's because of her. I went out with Hannah, and when I came back, she told the movers who brought our furniture where she wanted everything to go."

He takes off his suit. "Well, why not just tell the movers where you wanted it to go when you got home?"

"They had another job across town. They couldn't stay. I tried to get them to. I had all my plans written out and she changed everything the way she wanted it."

"Well, like you said, you were out. Did you tell her where you wanted everything?"

I breathe out. "Not exactly, but she knew about my notebook where I wrote it down."

He looks at me, puzzled. "Why did you even leave when you knew the movers were coming? I mean, all of this seems so petty."

"Petty?" I repeat. "I haven't gotten to the worst part of it. She invited me out to brunch with her friends."

"Oh, well, that's great, right?"

I put up my hands, pleading with him or let me finish. "I've never felt so embarrassed in my life. She joked that I may have daddy issues because my father passed away in prison! She even said she suspected I'd be a thief or a drug addict given who my father was. Her and her stupid friends laughed and laughed about my life. It was the worst, Leo. I literally took a taxi home. I couldn't go back to that table with your mother and those ladies. I couldn't go back to them laughing at me again."

Leo takes a deep breath of his own, managing not to defend his mother for a change and seemingly listening to what I have to say. "I don't understand. Could there have been a misunderstanding? She has a terrible sense of humor." I suppose he's not finished defending his dear mother.

"No. She meant to embarrass me in front of her friends, and she succeeded."

He scratches his head. "Listen, I'm going to talk to her. I agree we need to set up a date of when she needs to find something new." He looks around the room and shakes his head. "Two months. I'll tell her two months and I'll make sure she's set up somewhere else."

I lower my head and want to cry. "I can't do it for two months. That's too much."

He sighs. "Okay, one month. I'm trying to work with you, I am. I didn't think I'd be leaving my workday of negotiating with lenders to come home and negotiate between my wife and my mother. This is a lot for me. Hell, it's a lot for my mom. Her house is going to be auctioned in the next few days. The house I grew up in. The house where her husband – my dad... Well, there's just a lot of emotion going on right now."

I sigh. "So because your mother is emotional I have to be the target of her abuse?"

He shakes his head. "What? No. Of course not. I'm just saying, this is a difficult situation."

"Why can't she just stay somewhere else while we sort out everything? A nice hotel in downtown Calgary. Something. Anything!"

He sighs again. "She's my mother, okay? She needs me right now. She needs us right now. I came home because I wanted to spend time with my wife and my mother. Have dinner. Break bread. We'll be like the natives and the pilgrims. Come together and eat and be happy."

I scoff. "And what happened to the natives after? They took their lands, just like your mother is taking my home."

He sighs again. "I'm back, and I want to have a nice time. There's too much tension here. Let's just ease up a bit, okay? Have a nice night. I brought some porterhouse steak from the butcher on the way home. Besides, I had a good day at work. Things are looking up financially. Even Charles is less worried than usual."

"Well, I'm happy for you and Charles," I say, unable to hide my tone.

He gives me a thin smile. "I was hoping, well, you know, trying with you again tonight."

I laugh. "I'll break bread with you and your mother since you came home early, but I don't care what the test says; nobody is having a smile on their face tonight."

CHAPTER 20

Hannah brings Leo's plate to the table where we sit in silence. "Thanks Hannah," my husband says as she puts the food in front of him. "Looks great."

Delores sits beside him and I'm across the table from them both. Leo picks up his fork and knife and cuts into the thick porterhouse steak. He nods with satisfaction when he sees the pink inside, just the way he likes it.

As he begins to dine, Delores and I do the same. I take a moment and glance at my mother-in-law as she does the same. We look back at our plates of food.

"More wine, dear," Delores demands of Hannah, even though the wine bottle and her glass are directly in front of her. Hannah does as asked until Delores gives her a cue to stop pouring. "How was work?" Delores asks her son.

"Another brutal day of meetings," he says. "But it's working out well. We're getting more backers. Charles is drinking less coffee and has less anxiety for a change." He laughs.

"That's great, dear," Delores says, taking a small bite of her steak. She makes a sour face. "Too rare for my liking."

"Mine is just perfect," Leo says. "Hannah makes a great steak. Even back when she worked with me at the old bachelor pad, she did great." He looks at me and smiles. I grin back.

Delores sighs. "Elephant in the room, isn't it? Are we not going to bother addressing it?"

Leo nods. "I'm fine with just eating my steak, Mom. Let's just enjoy each other's company."

"I'm not really enjoying this," Delores says. I nearly laugh. For once I agree with my mother-in-law. "Today shouldn't have gone down the way it did." She looks at me. "I didn't realize I hurt your feelings." For a moment I feel like an actual apology is going to come out of her mouth until her next few words spill out. "You're just a little too sensitive, dear. I wasn't trying to hurt your feelings." She takes another bite of her steak and makes another face as she swallows.

I roll my eyes, unable to stop myself. "Too sensitive? You made fun of the fact that my father's dead!"

"I was making a jest, darling," she says, defending herself.

Leo pats his mother's leg. "That seemed a bit too harsh, Mom. Let's just try and get along better, okay?"

Delores nearly throws her knife and fork at her plate. "You always, always take her side. You seriously think I'd treat my daughter-in-law in such a crude way? I would never! I've only been nice to you," she says, pointing a finger towards me, "and you've treated me rotten since I stepped inside your home."

"What are you talking about?" I shout back. In what world have I been anywhere near as terrible as she has been to me? Leo raises his hand to try and plead with me to stop, but it's too late. His mother opened this can of worms.

Delores looks back at her son. "Do you see the tone she has? How she talks to me? She's been like this nearly the entire time. She has so much resentment toward me, and for what? I'm sorry I want grandkids! I'm sorry I went out of my way to show her around the community, meet some possible new friends, and take her to my favourite boutique." She looks at me with rage. "I've treated you well and you rub my face in dirt in return. Try and turn my only son against his mother!"

"Oh my god—" I bite my lip, but it doesn't help as more words escape my lips. "I'm not trying to do any of that. I just want you to be nice to me. You know even if you say mean things as a joke, it's still mean, right?"

She sighs. "Did your parents not teach you to speak to others with respect? Oh, I guess your father wouldn't have been able to, would he?"

I stand up, ready to walk away. "I can't believe her!"

"Mom!" Leo shouts. "That's her father you're talking about. Stop! Don't talk about her parents like that. What's wrong with you?"

"Taking her side, even though you can see how terrible she's been. I've listed all the nice things I've done for her, and she makes it abundantly clear I'm not welcome here. You will never take my side, will you? What have I done to you for you to not trust me when I tell you what happened?"

Leo lowers his head.

"Stop gaslighting your son!" I shout.

"Gaslighting?" Delores repeats in a tone that suggests she's never heard of the word.

"That's exactly what you're doing! Making him side with a reality that's made up in your head. Gaslighting!"

"Ha." She laughs. "I can't believe you're letting your wife talk to your mother this way." Delores reaches for her purse and takes out a cigarette. Before she can light it,

I point at her.

"Don't you dare light that cigarette, Delores!" I yell. "Smoke free house. How many times have—"

Leo strikes the table with his fist. I immediately sit down, and Delores jumps in fright. "Enough!" he shouts. He takes several deep breaths, before cutting into his steak and taking another bite. Before I can say a word, he turns his head toward the kitchen. "Hannah!"

She comes out reluctantly, taking small steps towards the table. "Is there something you need, sir? Something wrong?"

He wipes his mouth with a linen napkin. "This steak was cooked to perfection," he says in a tense voice. "Thank you for dinner. How about you leave early tonight?" She nods. "Maybe take a day off tomorrow. A paid day off. You deserve it for all the extra work you've been doing."

She glances at me a moment and back at my husband. "Thanks, Mr. Sterling. Leo, I mean. Thanks." I watch as she quickly gathers her things and leaves through the front door. How jealous I am of her, wishing I was anywhere but here.

Leo takes another bite of his steak before finally addressing me and his mother. He clears his throat and takes a sip of wine. He looks at me first, then his mother, before cutting into the steak forcefully. "You two *will* get along."

CHAPTER 21

We lay in our bed, but no words have been spoken between us. Essentially no words have been said since Hannah left. Each of us went to our own areas of the mansion, quiet for a change. When nighttime came, I was the first to go into our bedroom and change for bed. Soon after, Leo came. He didn't bother changing into night clothes and instead slipped right into the covers, his back turned to me.

I've been staring at his back, attempting to find the right words to say that will make all the tension stop. I've been replaying the meal we shared over and over since it happened.

It was as if someone lit a fuse and all three of us exploded at the table. Leo losing his cool is what stopped Delores and me in our tracks. Had he not been there, I'm not sure what would have happened. Likely Delores and I wouldn't have been "breaking bread" as Leo calls it.

After the last two meals I've shared with Delores, I don't think there will be many more planned ones with my mother-in-law.

That's something that's been playing in my mind over and over again as well. Delores isn't some random woman. She's my husband's mother. Even when she moves out, she will always be a part of our life. Leo will not stop talking to her. How much did my antics at the table hurt my husband? He's in the middle of all of this.

I can't control the things Delores says or does, but I can control how I react to them.

I've tried to sleep, but the fight at dinner keeps replaying in my mind. I can't go to sleep knowing my husband is upset with me.

I rub Leo's back, but he doesn't move. I'm worried that he's fallen asleep when he finally mutters a word. "Yeah," he says coldly.

"I'm sorry," I say, squeezing his shoulder. "I took that too far."

"No kidding," he says. "I'm not sure what I thought would happen if I came home and the three of us shared a meal. I guess, even in my wildest dreams, it wasn't ever like what just happened. I'm so embarrassed. Upset. I don't even know what I am right now. I just wish that never happened."

"Me too," I admit. "I was being aggressive, like you said. I was hurt. What she said at the golf course. Some of the comments she made since staying here. I took it all too personally. You said it will be just a month, and I know you'll keep your word."

He finally turns to me. "I need you to do better with this. Her house goes up for auction soon. The lawyers are working with the insurance company. Soon she'll have whatever money she can get, and I'll help her figure out her next steps in life. Until then, just make my life easier, please. I have this big business venture going on. A few missteps and my company could explode. I don't need this extra stress. I just don't need it."

"I'm sorry," I say again.

"If you can't control yourself around her, if you can't

be civil because of what she does or says, just walk away. But this house is certainly big enough for the two of you when I'm away."

"It is," I agree. "And I will walk away. I'll focus on moving the furniture how I want and decorating more. Hannah can help me. I'll stay busy."

"If you can't be in the same house, maybe just leave for a few hours. Maybe visit your mom tomorrow. Hannah won't be around. I won't be around. It's going to be a very long night at work for me tomorrow. After what happened tonight, I don't want you to be alone with my mom at home." He grabs my hand. "I just need you to get along with her, just for a little while."

I nod. "Well, you managed to do it nearly your whole life. I can do it for another few weeks." I laugh but he doesn't find me as funny. "I mean it, though," I assure him. "I'll do better." He kisses my hand and my lips before turning to his other side.

It's only a few weeks, I remind myself. It shouldn't be too hard to keep my promise.

CHAPTER 22

I can still feel the tension from last night when the sun rises the next day. Only, it's worse somehow. As Leo promised, he left early, and I knew he meant it when he said he wouldn't be back home until much later. I don't blame him. Who would want to come back to what happened last night?

I still get upset, mostly at myself, for how it went. Delores was my fuse and I exploded given the tiny wick I had left with her. I've always felt I'm a very calm and collected person. I don't believe I've ever raised my voice at someone before, except maybe my own mother when I was in that rebellious teenager stage.

Delores is enough to make any woman go mad, but I gave my word to my husband. I will do better and I mean it. That means a cooling off period. It was a rather good idea of my husband's. No matter how huge my house is, at this exact moment in time, it doesn't feel large enough for both of us.

I'll keep myself busy the next few days. I'll stay out of the house completely if I have to. With her home being auctioned, I suppose Delores will be busy herself. Maybe she'll leave as well and will do me the favor of not having to myself.

Eventually, when things calm down, we can attempt

to share words again without them being with raised voices. It is true what they say. Time heals all. At least I hope so. As little as I make a month sound to myself, it's still thirty days. Within that timeframe, we'll still be in the same house and see each other.

Today, I won't worry about that, though. I have a mission. Leave this house for an extended period of time until I feel comfortable coming back. Hannah won't be here today. My husband graciously gave her a day off.

She deserves it. She's been putting up with just as much abuse from Delores as me. The way she subtly bosses her around would be irritating to deal with. Hannah and I would joke about our terrible clients when we worked homes together. A woman like Delores Sterling would give us plenty of material to talk about at lunch breaks.

I think about calling Hannah to spend the day together. It would be nice to hang out like old times, outside of this house without all the tension that comes with it. I pick up my cell and I'm about to call her when I change my mind.

I'm not just her friend anymore. I'm her employer. Does she really want to hang around with me outside of work on her day off? Wasn't last night enough for her? She likely needs her own cooling off period herself away from my house and not only Delores but me as well.

My husband did have another great idea last night. Visit my mom. She's hours away. A drive to her home and back in one day would take an entire day. If I want to, I can even stay the night. Spend some quality time with my mom.

Besides, I have a box full of things Leo was thinking of donating that my mom may enjoy. I think she'll get a kick out of the Google speakers. She can ask it to play her favourite songs as she does chores. I left the box under one of the lower kitchen cabinets.

Leo will be busy the next few days anyway. I can stay in my old room. I look around my new bedroom and remind myself where I started. My bedroom was a quarter of the size of my current walk-in closet. I shake my head at how crazy life can be.

One day I'm cleaning homes, and the next I live in a mansion and have my own cleaners.

Delores certainly thinks it's funny. So do her rich friends. I catch myself before I head down another resentful memory exercise about how annoying my mother-in-law can be.

I call my mom and she picks up immediately. "Hey!" she says enthusiastically.

"Hey, Mom. I was thinking of stopping by for a visit."

"Today?" she asks, surprised.

"Yeah, I thought it would be nice to catch up."

"Of course," she says. Even though I'm not in the room with her, I can tell she's smiling. "Should I make your old bed? You're not going to drive all the way to Edmonton and back home, are you?"

"Maybe make my bed just in case," I say. Talking about my old bedroom makes me feel all cozy inside. "I'm about to leave so I'll see you in a few hours."

I smile as I get ready and think about my day. This is exactly what I need. Some time with people who I love and won't be at work all day, leaving me with their moms. I take another deep breath, again catching myself before I let my mind run through all the reasons I should be pissed off at the other woman living in my house right now.

As I walk down the hall I hear her voice in the

kitchen. Delores must be on the phone again. I quickly walk past and into the foyer, leaving through the front door. I get into my vehicle and turn the ignition fast like I'm breaking out of prison when it's actually my own home.

As I drive down toward the main road, I see Cero planting flowers in a small garden near the entrance to our property. I slow as I near the gate and Cero looks into my car. He always has such an intense gaze on him and it creeps me out at times.

The more I think of the man, the more I hope Hannah continues to stay away from him. I hit the button on my dashboard to open the gate. I wait for what feels like forever for it to open wide enough to drive through. I wave at Cero before I leave, and he nods in return.

I stop at a Starbucks for a venti mocha that's needed for the long road before hitting the highway. The first thirty minutes of my drive goes by fast. Having finished my mocha some time ago, I consider stopping to get a second along the highway somewhere.

Suddenly it hits me. The box. The items I wanted to give to my mom are still in the kitchen. I think about whether to just keep driving, but a ramp is quickly coming up ahead. Last minute, I get off the highway and back onto it again, going the opposite way. I want to stretch out today as long as I can. A ride back home will help with that. I don't mind it so much. Besides a quick bathroom break and another mocha sounds about right.

Unfortunately, the ride back feels like it's taking twice as long as leaving. It gives me enough time to think about everything that's been happening.

I think of my conversation with Hannah the other day when she asked what I thought of my father-in-law's death. I think of the odd investigator, Tony Cardone. I glance at my purse and put it in my lap, taking quick moments to search around inside until I find it.

I take out his card. For a moment I wonder what would happen if I called him. I still have so many questions. Why would he think it was anything else besides a suicide? Is there more to the story than I know? There has to be something for this man to have been following us and finally knocking at my door with questions.

I remember what my husband said just the night before. How I need to make his life easier right now. Also, don't talk to investigators. I put his card back into my purse and try my best not to think about it more, but it's hard.

Does the investigator really think my husband was involved in his father's death? If so, what would he have gained? He already knew he wasn't going to get much, if anything. His father told him to his face he was out of the will years ago. As for Delores, she got nothing from her husband's death. Her life is ruined. Her home is being auctioned. Her lifestyle will be forever changed.

Thankfully, I make it back home before my mind wanders further. I press the button in my car to open the gate, and I'm even more thankful that Cero isn't there to greet me with his awkwardly long stares.

I park outside and take a deep breath as I walk up the steps to my house. I'm taken back by how nervous I am going into my own home. I never thought I'd have such a sensation. With any luck, Delores is in her room and I can quickly go to the bathroom and grab the box from the kitchen.

I open the front door quietly, as if I'm an intruder in

my own house. It's dead quiet. If it wasn't for Delores's Rolls-Royce parked outside, I'd question if she was even here.

Suddenly I hear a shriek. My heart stops, questioning what I just heard. Then I hear her.

"No! Stop!" It's coming from the hall towards Delores's room. I take out my phone. I'm not sure if I should run out and call the police or run into my mother-in-law's room to help, but from the sound of her voice I know something terrible is happening inside her bedroom.

I quietly step towards it, my phone gripped in my palm, when I again hear her call out. "No! Don't stop!" This time her voice sounds more lighthearted, playful even. She even laughs. Then I hear the loud moans of a man.

My eyes widen as I realize what I'm hearing. The man laughs. "Mamacita, you go too hard on a man."

"No fun, darling," I hear Delores laugh. "I thought you young men had mileage for days in you."

"Twice today already, mama," the man says.

I don't have to open the door to know who it is. It's obvious from his accent. My body shakes with disgust.

Cero Rivera is in my mother-in-law's bedroom.

CHAPTER 23

"Another round, darling?" Delores says between laughs.

I cry inside at the thought of what's happening inside my guest room. The door is partially open, and I can hear the flick of Delores's lighter. She is no doubt having a cigarette after a sexual marathon with our gardener.

"Esparer." Cero laughs. "Wait. Wait."

I start to slowly back down the hall, praying the floor doesn't creak, giving off my position again. The last thing I want is for my mother-in-law to know I've caught her with her lover.

Lover. The idea of if makes me sick. Cero does have wandering eyes, but I never thought they were on Delores. I can almost feel my Starbucks coffee about to come back up my throat. I take a few more steps before I can hear more movement coming from the bedroom followed by more hushed moans from both of them. I start to move faster down the hall. I turn my head to look back at my guest room and can feel the anger I have about what's happening in the room.

When I turn back, I jump in shock to find Charles Rayer again staring back at me.

"Sorry," he says shyly. "The doorbell is broken. Is—"

"Leo isn't here," I say with a cold tone. A sudden loud

moan from Delores draws both of our attention down the hall. Charles looks nearly as disgusted as I feel. "Do yourself a favor: run away from this house," I tell him. I walk past him and back out the front door. I start my car and drive as fast as I can down the driveway. If I could ram through my gate to allow me to leave faster I would, but instead I wait for what feels like forever.

When I left this morning, Cero was awkwardly watching me as I waited for the gate to fully open. I'm starting to realize why he looked so creepily at me, watching me as I left.

The minute I was down the road, he likely ran into my home and started the fun and games with my mother-in-law. In. My. Home.

Thank god Delores brought her own bed set. If it was my furniture, I'd have to set it ablaze.

I try my best to get the sounds of their pleasure out of my mind, but it's impossible. I feel like I can hear every movement, every slight sound of pleasure escaping their lips, as if I was in the room with them.

Why won't my brain stop tormenting me? I accelerate. I have a long drive ahead of me. I didn't even grab the box from the kitchen that I originally went back for. I don't even go back to Starbucks, and I still have to go to the bathroom.

Ugh.

Why did I have to go back? I feel like I can never go back to my home ever again now.

Poor Charles. I left him in the hallway. I didn't even look back to see if he ran from the house as I had. I couldn't stay a moment more in my own home.

I'm certain I'm staying the night at my mother's now. I can't go back there. Not after what I heard. Hearing it almost feels worse than seeing it as my brain is coming up with all sorts of ideas and positions of what they were doing inside the bedroom.

My body shakes at the thought of it.

How long have the two of them been having their fun together? I pray it was the first time, but somehow I know better. Cero was Delores's gardener for years. They had plenty of opportunities for round after round of sex while Leonard Sterling wasn't home.

My father-in-law worked his entire life. He lived at his office. Delores could have been having an affair for years.

I remember how Delores was talking to someone on the phone and asked them to not call right now. It seems obvious who she was talking to now. Her lover, Cero.

I did it again. I said *lover* and my brain instantly torments me with the moans from my mother-in-law that will forever be stuck in my brain.

Delores did not want Cero to call her after everything that happened with her husband. Who would want their affair to become public after their husband killed himself?

As I drive to my mom's home, I continue to go over everything that I witnessed. I question why Tony Cardone thought my husband could be behind his father's death. I didn't understand how he could have a motive. He hadn't gotten along with his father for years. That was nothing new.

I thought the same when it came to Delores as well. What motive could she have to kill her own husband and stage it as a suicide? It didn't make sense. She received no money after Leonard's death.

With Cero dramatically entering the picture, it suddenly does. A motive has now come to the forefront. I glance at my purse. Buried somewhere inside it is Tony's card.

    I take a deep breath and look outside. First, I have to go to the bathroom.

CHAPTER 24

I sit in the small cafeteria of a highway rest stop. I'm nearly halfway to my mom's house. Instead of finishing my drive, I've sat at this table for nearly thirty minutes now. I'm starting to get worried that one of the workers will ask me to leave and not loiter here.

I'm frozen.

All I can do is stare at my cell phone in the center of the table, with Tony Cardone's card below it.

Every time I get close to picking up my cell to call him, I put it back down. I feel like once I do call him, there's no going back.

On one side of my conscience, I hear Leo's voice telling me not to talk to investigators. On the other hand, I think about the implications of an affair between Delores and Cero on Tony's investigation into my father-in-law's death.

I remind myself that he's not even a detective. He's not a cop. He's just an insurance agent who doesn't want to cut a check for my mother-in-law. He's representing his company, not me. He doesn't care about the truth. He wants enough reasonable doubt to protect his company from having to pay whatever the life insurance amount is.

I shouldn't even be considering calling him. The

longer the investigation takes, the longer Delores will be in my home. What if my information changes everything, though? What if Delores finds out that I called Tony? What if my husband finds out?

I shake my head and continue to stare at my phone. I remind myself how terrible it's been living with Delores.

In my moment of rage, I grab my phone and dial his number before I can think about my actions. I almost feel relief when I hear my phone ringing. Then the anxiety hits me and I'm scared if he picks up.

"Cardone," he says. He even sounds like a detective when he answers his phone.

"This is Mrs. Sterling. Madelyn Sterling."

"Oh, yes. Hello. How can I help you?"

I can almost hear my husband's voice pleading with me not to tell him anything that could make everything more complicated.

"Why do you think Leonard Sterling's death was not suicide?" I finally manage to ask him.

There's a brief pause. "Why did you feel the need to call me today?" he asks.

I breathe in deep and consider telling him about Delores's affair with Cero. Then again, maybe it wasn't an affair. It could have easily happened after Leonard Sterling killed himself. Sex is a decent way to get over grieving. Hannah even joked about that. Then again, I don't think I've seen Delores shed a tear for her former husband.

"You first," I say, not budging. "I'm not going—"

"DPI," he says, cutting me off.

"What was that?" I say, confused.

"DPI. It's an abbreviation for dots per inch. It's a technical term a printer's print quality. The higher the

DPI, the better the quality."

I take a deep breath. "I don't understand."

"Leonard Sterling left a suicide note. It was printed. Not a handwritten note. He actually printed his supposed last words. That was my first red flag. Second was the DPI of the note. I had our lab analyze the printed note. It was printed off a low-quality printer. In Leonard Sterling's home office, the DPI is 1200. The DPI of the suicide note was 300. That's a four-times difference from the printer at his home."

I've never heard this term before in my life and now my entire world feels like it's spinning because of it. "So what does this mean?"

"It doesn't add up," Cardone says. "First, a man plans to kill himself and prints off a suicide note? Was he worried his last words would be ineligible? Then the DPI isn't of the same quality of the printer he uses on a frequent basis. So, what, he went somewhere else and printed off a suicide note just to bring it back home? It doesn't make sense."

"What do the police think? How come they're not taking this seriously?"

He gives an audible scoff. "They just wanted to close a case. Easy one for them. A man was found dead at his home. A suicide note was found beside him. Gun residue found on his fingers."

I laugh. "Gun residue on Leonard's fingers. Of course the police will think he did it to himself."

"Ah. There was a second bullet shot into the wall. Whoever killed him with the first bullet could have used the old man's finger to pull the trigger. And what, did Leonard Sterling somehow manage to miss shooting himself in the head?"

"Maybe he had second thoughts in his last moment."

He laughs. "That's what the police say too."

I breathe out. "And you think my husband or mother-in-law is involved?"

"I'm just asking questions, ma'am. The question of did he actually kill himself seems answered to me. Who did it is the question I have now."

"But the police still aren't taking this seriously," I say. "Why? I just can't see them not taking the death of one of the richest men in the country seriously."

"They're not the ones who have to pay out his life insurance. I'm the only one who sees something is off. I know it in my heart. I need more evidence though… So why did you call me?"

I breathe out. For what feels like a lifetime, I don't reply. I can still hear Leo in my ear. I can still hear his voice as if he's here beside me saying there could be other reasons that explain everything. The fact that only one man, an insurance man who has an interest in not paying out the life insurance, is the only one not convinced should tell me something. He's holding up the whole process for Delores because of this.

"You scared me," I finally manage to answer. And it's true. Since Tony revealed himself at my front door, I have continued to think of what he said and the feelings I felt.

"Nothing else?" he says. "I don't believe you. What is it?"

"You're insinuating that I'm living with a murderer," I say. "I'm scared and need to know more. I need to know why you thought my father-in-law's death wasn't what the police told us." I can feel my heart beating faster as if it's about to explode out of my chest. Talking about this makes my stomach curl. It's beyond frightening.

He laughs. "You need to tell me. I'm one of the only people you can trust right now. The fact is you *are* living with a murderer. What happens when they find out you're—"

I quickly hang up the phone. I can't bear to hear more. I slide my phone across the table and wish I never called the investigator. Suddenly it begins to buzz on the table, inching its way closer to me with each vibration. In a panic, I grab it and turn it off entirely.

CHAPTER 25

When I arrive at my mom's house, I nearly fall into her arms when she opens her door. Even though I'm in my twenties, knowing that my mom is there to support me just makes everything a little bit easier.

She can tell by my wet eyes that something is wrong. I tell her the minimum. Delores moved in with us and it's been difficult. Understatement of the century. There's a lot more to it than just that. I won't talk about my father-in-law's inheritance. I certainly won't say a word about Tony Cardone's investigation.

If I did, my mom would never let me leave. Part of me doesn't want to. The heavy feeling in my chest that I've had the past several days in my own home lifted as soon as I stepped into my mom's.

Staying in my old bedroom that I had as a child makes it even more comforting. The world is scary out there, but here, I feel safe.

We sit at my mom's small dining table having tea. I don't even have to ask; Mom makes it for me out of routine. We used to sit at this table for hours talking to one another. Today is the same. We sit and chat about nothing, and I love it.

Given how I was when I arrived, though, Mom has many questions, many of which I skirt around. I don't want her to know how messed up things are in my life. I don't want her to know any of the troubles I'm having. I honestly just want to be around her, and doing so makes me feel so much better.

"Things with Leo okay?" she says. I knew she would eventually ask how much of my current situation was down to Leo.

"It's been a little tough, yeah," I admit. "It's more my mother-in-law, though."

"Delores." She shakes her head. "I remember how it was when your father passed away. I had a really hard time with it. I didn't think I'd make it on my own without help. Somehow I managed to scrounge up enough money to keep paying for this house and raise you in it. I had to work several jobs to make it work, but I did." She smiles. "It's nothing like what you have now. You won't have to worry about money like I did."

I sigh. "That's true." It's something I've been thinking a lot about, ever since I moved into my new home and since Delores became my new roommate. "You know, Mom, I know we didn't have much, but I want you to know how much love I felt in this house. We had barely enough to make it, but we had each other."

She smiles, but part of me remembers feeling different as a child. I remember not having nice clothes, some even with holes in them. I remember being made fun of at grade school because my shoes were worn out and dirty. It felt like we really had nothing. We would get groceries from food drives. I knew the schedule for where we could get charitable donations better than my mom. I recall mid-March one year when I told Mom that there was a spring/summer clothing giveaway for struggling families. I knew the clothes would be brand new instead of used, and for a change I wanted to be the first person to wear my new shoes, or sweater, or anything that was mine. We went to the event and I remember how upset I was at not finding much that might fit me except an oversized pair of pants. Thankfully it was at a time where loose clothes were popular and most kids didn't notice.

I think about my husband. Despite his family having enough money to do whatever they desired, Leo would tell me how depressed he was growing up. His father wasn't around. Where my father was behind bars for making money illegally, his was never home, making much more money legally.

Leo had only his mother with him. Knowing what I know of her, I can only imagine what that was like.

"What I'm trying to say," my mom says, breaking me out of my thoughts, "is Delores is going through a lot. She lost her husband. She was married to him much longer than I was with your father. I can only imagine what that would be like. You told me that it was her who found him as well?" I nod and my mother takes a deep breath. "How terrible. That woman must be going through a lot right now."

For a moment, I want to tell her not to worry for a woman like Delores Sterling. She appears to have moved on to her former landscaper for some extra attention right now. I don't, though.

I grab Mom's hand and squeeze it. "I loved living in this house with you. Maybe I didn't think that when I was growing up, but we had a lot of love here. I think about my life now, and that beautiful home I live in, and right this second, I could care less. Give me a house like this with Leo and a few kids, and I'd be just as happy."

My mom gives a thin smile. "You won't have nearly

the same struggles I had raising you with Leo, though. He's a smart businessman and with him providing for you and my future grandchildren, you will have a beautiful family who never have to worry."

My phone buzzes. I notice it's Leo. I also notice the time. It's nearly nine at night. I hadn't called or texted to let him know where I was. I pick up the phone immediately.

"Hey," Leo says with a soft tone. "I was worried about you."

I stand up from the table and move to the living room area. The small house has an open concept design, but it's tiny. Even though my mom is staring right at me and can hear every word I say, I feel like I have more privacy here.

"Hey," I say back. "Sorry, it's been a day."

Leo sounds off. Not as upbeat as he usually is. It can't just be because that I'm not home. Did Charles tell my husband about Delores and Cero? This day has been difficult enough that I don't want to go there right now.

"Where are you?" he asks.

"I took your advice. I'm spending the night with my mom. Take a little break from my own home."

He sighs. "Did my mom do something again?"

Oh, she did something, I think. I bite my lip. I realize that Leo must not know about his mother and Cero. I can't tell him something like this over the phone. When I see him, I'll tell him everything.

"When are you going to come home?" he asks.

I pause again before answering. "Soon," I say. "I just wanted to spend time with Mom. It feels like it's been a while."

"Okay," he says reluctantly. "You are coming back though, right?"

"I am, yeah."

"Well, I do have good news for you. I spoke with my lawyer today. The insurance company will be cutting a check to my mom. The life insurance money is on its way. This will be over soon. Then we can focus on us again."

While I'm overwhelmed with happiness, part of me is upset. I spoke with Tony this morning and he never said a word about this change with the insurance company.

It hits me. Tony Cardone was using me for information. A last-ditch effort to not give my mother-in-law what was owed to her. He messed with my head to try and get something out of me. What would have happened if I told him about the affair with Cero? That could have delayed them paying Delores, which was exactly what Tony wanted.

I can feel myself flush red at the idea.

"So, are you coming home?" Leo asks.

"Tomorrow."

CHAPTER 26

I leave my mom's house after lunch the next day. I know Leo will be at work late and don't want to go home too early. The last thing I want is to be alone for a long time with Delores. I know her secret and still don't know what to do with it.

Telling Leo seems like the only right thing to do. Then again, I don't want to involve myself in this more than I have to. What my mother-in-law does behind closed doors is not something I want to inject myself into.

Then again, the conversation I had with Tony Cardone still plays in my head. After our talk yesterday, I was scared, fearful that my father-in-law's death was not what it seemed. Then I find out through my husband that the insurance company is paying Delores. That wouldn't happen if there was credible evidence that his suicide was still questionable.

So why didn't Tony tell me they were going to pay her when I spoke with him yesterday? Don't talk to police or investigators, my husband warned me.

I feel so stupid.

I've been driving for the past few hours playing over in my mind how dumb I've been.

In a fit of anger, I pull over to the side of the highway and take out my cell, dialing Tony's number. "Cardone," he says again in his fake detective voice.

"Mr. Cardone," I say to him in a harsh tone of my own. "Madelyn Sterling."

"I'm glad you called. Have you thought more about what you wanted to say to me yesterday?"

"No," I answer curtly. "I want to know why your insurance company is paying my mother-in-law the policy amount if you think my father-in-law was murdered?" There's a long pause on the phone. "That's what I thought. You slimy insurance people! You had me thinking all sorts of things all night about who I was living with."

"You should be afraid," he says coldly. "He did not kill himself."

"Then why did you pay the life insurance?"

He pauses again. "If it was my decision, we wouldn't have paid a cent."

I laugh. "Of course," I say. 'Insurance company trying to weasel their way out of paying what is owed.' Not a new story, is it?"

"It's not that," he says. "I know in my heart that Leonard Sterling did not kill himself. I told you about—"

"DPI," I say. "Yes, but really, all you have is dots per inch from a printer."

"The DPI of Leonard Sterling's home computer did not match the one used on the suicide note. Same for his office printer. The employee from the home office store confirmed it. So where did he print the suicide note?"

For a moment, I hold my breath, trying to ensure I heard his words correctly. "Did you say a home office store? When we talked yesterday you told me that you analyzed the suicide note through your lab. Some pimple-faced teenager at a retail store is your lab?"

"There isn't exactly a lab for this," he says confidently. "And the employee who helped me was at least eighteen."

I laugh. "The kid probably thought you were going to buy a printer from him. You lied to him as well! You lied to me. I can't trust anything you say."

"So why did you call me?" he asks. "There's something more here, and you know it. Otherwise, you wouldn't be on the phone with me at all, would you? What are you not telling me?"

I shake my head and bang on my steering wheel, causing my horn to beep. "I'm calling to let you know that I know you're full of it. I should have listened to my husband and never talked to you. I made a mistake by listening to your lies. You want to talk to me again? Call my lawyer!" I hang up my cell and bang on my steering wheel again.

CHAPTER 27

When I get to the gates of my property, I quickly look around and thankfully don't see Cero anywhere. I don't think I could look him in the eye right now knowing what I do. I head down the drive and as I do, I see him.

Cero's trimming a bush nearby. He glances in my direction but quickly looks away.

I park and notice Delores's Rolls-Royce isn't there. My lucky day so far. No awkward looks from Cero and my mother-in-law is nowhere in sight. The fact that he's still cutting our bushes is a good indicator Leo doesn't know what Cero and his mother have been up to. I wonder what he'll do when he finds out.

Another sign of my lucky day, Hannah's car is here.

I get inside quickly, not looking back out of fear of catching Cero's attention. I look around but can't find Hannah. I look in the kitchen for her but she's not there either, nor on Delores's side of the house.

"Hannah?" I call out. "Are you here?" Talking to her will make me feel better. I need to decompress to someone and since she already knows most of everything that's going on, I may as well disclose the rest. I didn't feel comfortable talking to my mom. She would get too concerned for me. Hannah will be more objective.

I hear some sounds coming from upstairs. Hannah

walks slowly down the spiral staircase.

"Hey," I called out. "There you are."

She has two small boxes in her hands and nearly drops one when she misses a step. "Hey," she says back. "I seriously hate these steps. I was wondering where you were."

I wait until she comes down fully before I hug her. "How was your day off?"

"Great and well needed," she says. "I did absolutely nothing and loved every moment of it. I can only imagine how it was when I left."

I smile. "I just came back from my mom's house. I spent the night. I had to get out of this house too after that dinner."

"What happened after I left?"

"I don't even know where to start," I answer. I put a hand to my head. "The past twenty-four hours have been intense."

"Well, start with the juiciest part," Hannah jokes.

"You love this, don't you?"

"Rich people problems? Yes, I do." She laughs again.

I look outside the window and confirm Cero is nowhere near us. "Well for one thing, my mother-in-law may have been having an affair with our landscaper."

Hannah's mouth drops open. "Cero?"

I tell her how my day started yesterday. How I found Cero in Delores's bedroom and the terrible sounds of pleasure that came from them.

"What a scumbag," Hanna says, shaking her head. "I made the mistake of giving him my number and he hit me up on my day off, wanting to get together. I said no, and now I'm glad I did."

I make a face. "You did yourself a favor. I'm not

sure how long they've been a 'thing'. Maybe it was the first time, maybe it's been something long term. How do I know? It made me think about that insurance investigator." I can't hide my guilty face.

"Oh no," she says. "What did you do?"

"I called the insurance guy." I tell her what Tony Cardone told me. I have never used the term "DPI" as much as I have in the last two days. I tell her how I found out through Leo afterwards that the insurance company is paying Delores. "So she may not be here much longer."

Hannah smiles. "Thank god."

"Where is she today?"

"She doesn't exactly talk to me," Hannah says. "Only when she wants something do I exist." She shakes her head. "I still don't get why this insurance guy feels so strongly about the suicide. Just because of the DPN."

"DPI," I correct her.

"Whatever. DPI. His whole idea is that he wouldn't have planned his own suicide by printing out a note somewhere else? That's it? I mean, I knew a guy from high school who, you know, and before he did it, he threw a party. He called his friends. Gave some of his things away to people. He planned his death for weeks. He even tried to call me."

"He called you?"

Hannah nods. "I didn't pick up. I'm so happy I did not know what he intended to do. Next thing you know, I find out he killed himself. So, people definitely do plan their suicide. Even if the letter was printed somewhere else, that doesn't matter, at least I think."

"I suppose that's what the police think too, which is why they're not talking to Leo about DPI or anything stupid like that. There was also a second bullet fired that day," I tell her. "Cardone thinks that because there was a second shot fired that it shows someone killed Leonard Sterling and used his hand to fire a second bullet so that the gun residue would show on my father-in-law's fingers."

Hannah raises an eyebrow. "I suppose that's interesting but maybe he had second thoughts about what he was doing."

I lower my head and take a deep breath. "That was my thinking, too."

"You want my opinion?" she asks. "I don't think your mother-in-law had anything to do with her husband's death. Whatever happened with Cero, who cares? Has nothing to do with anything. Rich people doing scandalous things. So what?"

I laugh. "I was thinking of telling Leo about Cero. His business partner walked into the house too and heard Delores and Cero. I don't think he told him either."

"You want my advice?" she asks. "Don't get involved. She's about to leave your home. Let her do her thing. You do you. Also, don't talk to this Tony guy again. He's definitely playing you."

Before I can say a word, the front door opens and Delores walks in. She gives a thin smile to both Hannah and me.

"Afternoon, dear," she says to me.

"Hey, Delores," I say.

She nods at Hannah and back at me. "I, ummm, well, there's no easy way to say this... I'm sorry." Her apology surprises me. Before I can ask why, she continues. "I've been a difficult person to live with. Not an ideal roommate, I know. You and I are family now. I don't know if Leo told you, but I'll be getting the life insurance money soon. I'll be out of your hair entirely."

I glance at Hannah, who seems nearly as shocked as me. "I'll finish unpacking this box," she says, before walking down the hall.

I wonder how much of her apology was because of something Leo said to her last night when I was at my mom's home. He must have talked her into it. Still though, for a change she comes off as genuine. No *dear* or *darling*. No double talk where she says something mean in a nice way.

Only an apology.

"What are you doing right now?" she asks. "How about we grab some coffee? I want to show you this wonderful place nearby."

I take a moment before answering. Part of me still wants to avoid her like the plague but the other side of me realizes that I've been hard on her as well. I can't believe the thoughts I had in my head last night. I know for sure that I can't trust what Tony Cardone says.

I thought my mother-in-law was the worst. Maybe she did something to her husband. The thought of it made it hard to sleep.

"That sounds wonderful," I say.

CHAPTER 28

Delores drives into the parking lot of Foothills Firearm Center. I look at her confused.

"I thought we were going for coffee?" I say.

"We are, darling," she says with a wicked smile. "And to skeet shoot. You'll absolutely love it. There's something about watching something explode and knowing you destroyed it that makes you feel alive." Her grin widens.

She opens the door and steps out. I sit in her car and wonder what I was thinking to ever agree to go out with my mother-in-law again. Somehow we've ended up in a place where she'll be alone with me with a gun in her hand. I look at the small gun center and hear the sounds of nearby shots. I realize I'm not exactly alone.

I step out of the car while Delores closes her trunk. In her hands is a large shotgun. She smiles at me. "I'll rent one for you, dear, don't worry. We won't share. When I go with my skeet club girls, we never share a shotgun. It's bad luck."

"Okay," I say with a weary smile. "I just didn't think we'd be coming here today."

She laughs. "I thought it would be a nice way to loosen up, dear. Things have been so tense between us. Maybe letting off some steam together would be best. You'll thank me for this later. Who knows, maybe you'll get your own gun someday."

She turns and walks into the building. I reluctantly follow her. When I enter, she's already speaking to the cashier, filling out a form. I stand behind her.

"Which shotgun would you like to try, dear?" Delores asks. "My personal favourite is one like mine. It only has two rounds you can fire at a time though."

I smile at the cashier. "Same as hers, I guess." The cashier turns around and grabs a shotgun from the rack. She hands it to me, and I grab it as if it's infected with a contagious disease. This is my first time ever touching something so powerful. I'm uneasy at first.

Delores laughs. "Don't worry, darling. It's not loaded, of course."

"Would you like some shells today, Ms. Sterling?" the cashier asks.

"No, dear, " she says with enthusiasm. "I always bring my own." She pats her designer purse. She turns her head to a nearby table with confectionery on it and a coffee pot. "Oh, I nearly forgot, and two coffees."

As we sip our coffees, I follow Delores outside to the range. The air is crisp, and the sound of weapons being discharged echoes around us.

Delores finishes her coffee and throws it in a trash bin near one of the gun lanes. It almost feels like I'm at a golf range, only firing weapons instead of hitting balls.

Delores was absolutely wrong about one thing. The coffee here is complete garbage. I have barely a few sips before throwing my cup in the bin along with hers.

Delores opens the shotgun. She takes a small carton full of shells out of her purse. "It's really not too hard, dear," she says. "Two slots. Two shells go in them, just like this." She slides in two cartridges. "Then close it." She whips her hand back and the barrel of the shotgun wizzes backwards until it clicks, locking it.

She smiles at me. "Now, the best part." She nods behind me. "See that joystick thing? Grab it and click the button whenever I say pull. A clay disc will be shot out, and…" She raises the gun towards the skyline. "Fire at will. You've got two tries to hit it. If you hit the disc with your first round, you can attempt to hit another with your second. Then, we switch places. I'll click the button for you and you fire." She turns the shotgun to the side. "This is the safety. When it's on, you can't fire the gun." She clicks the switch and smiles at me. "Now, it's not so safe. Does that make sense, darling?" I nod. "Oh, and don't forget to put on your earmuffs. They look silly but its better to wear it when firing. One of my girlfriends didn't put hers on in time and now has tinnitus, poor girl."

We both put on our earmuffs, and I step back towards the button, waiting for her to yell.

"Pull," she says. I click the button and a disc shoots out. Delores fires at it, missing, but when she fires next, the clay disc explodes in the air. My heart palpitates at the sight. I have to admit, it is exciting to watch. I'm a little nervous to try, though.

"I'm a little rusty," Delores says. "Missed that first shot. Your turn, dear."

We change positions. Delores is at my back. Her shotgun is sitting on a rack beside the button.

I shuffle the gun in my hand until it feels comfortable wedged against my shoulder. I try my best to have good posture like Delores showed me.

"Everything okay, dear?" she asks.

I breathe in deep. "Pull!"

Suddenly a disc shoots out and within a second,

I breathe out, pulling the trigger. The clay disc immediately explodes.

Delores claps behind me. "Well done, darling. First time lucky."

She was absolutely right. I feel so powerful right now, like I could conquer the world, all because I destroyed a clay disc. I laugh to myself and yell for her to pull again. The second disc shoots out and I fire but miss this time.

"Can't get them all, dear," Delores says. She loads her shotgun, and we change positions again. I place my shotgun on the rack and wait for my mother-in-law to say the word. When she yells "pull" I click the button immediately and almost as quickly, Delores strikes the disc. She yells for me to release the second one and she hits her target again.

I laugh and clap my hands just as Delores did for me. Only when Delores turns to me, her face sours. As she turns, the barrel of the gun is directed at my chest. Smoke comes from it. She gives me a thin smile. Panic hits me as her smile grows and becomes more wicked in nature. I remember that she fired her two rounds. The gun is empty. I try my best to breathe again. For a moment, I worry she'll load her gun and fire at me, given the expression on her face.

"You didn't have to tell my son," she says, lowering the barrel towards the ground.

"What do you mean?"

"Cero and I," she says. "You told my son about us. I think that's rather inappropriate."

I take a deep breath. "Listen, I heard you two the other day, but I didn't say anything to Leo. I went to my mom's house for a visit and just wanted to forget about everything I heard. It's none of my bus—"

"Business, darling. I agree. It's not your concern who I bed, is it? And yet my son knows my business."

I shake my head. "Charles. He came into the home looking for Leo. I left as he did. I know for a fact he heard you too."

"Charles?" Delores says, just as confused. "And yet I didn't see him in the house. I didn't see his car in the driveway. I did see you getting into your vehicle and leaving. Today I got a call from my son saying we need to talk."

"Whatever is going on with you and Cero is none of my business," I say again. "I wish I had never heard it, believe me."

She laughs. "I suppose you wouldn't want to know. You don't know what it was like being married to a man like Leonard Sterling. I see how my son treats you. He adores you. Loves you. Never in my forty-six years with Leonard did I feel a day of what you receive from my son. I get that from Cero, not that it's any of your business."

"It's not," I agree.

"And yet you want to ruin what I have with Cero." She walks past me and places her shotgun on the rack. "I never liked my mother-in-law. Leonard's mother was atrocious. From the day I met her until the day she began rotting in the ground, we disliked each other. If her corpse could still talk, she'd probably still be mean. I never thought I'd have that relationship with my own daughter-in-law. Then again, I never thought my son would marry a woman like you."

"What does that mean?"

She smiles. "Well, you're not like us, are you? You do well, fitting in the best you can. You aren't meant to live this lifestyle. You didn't earn it. You didn't grow into it.

You married into it. Tell me, when you started cleaning my son's house, did you see dollar bills in your eyes as you flirted with him? A bit of a fetish, isn't it? Sleeping with the maid? You used him. I never thought you had the best intentions for my son. Then I moved in with you and feel it even more so."

I take my shotgun from the rack. "I always wanted to get along with my future mother-in-law too. I never thought it would be like this. It didn't have to be. Today, for a moment, I thought we were getting along. Now, I see through you."

"You do, dear?"

"I do." I load the shotgun and snap back the barrel. Delores raises her eyebrows, unable to hide how impressed she is with how quickly I've picked up on her hobby. "I married your son because I love him. If he made a fraction of what he currently makes, I'd be by his side. Sometimes, after living with you, I wish he was poor. I see what money does to families. What it's done to yours."

"I gave my son everything I could!" Delores shouts. For a moment I catch her glancing at her shotgun. The instinctive part of me almost wishes she would grab it to test me. I can feel my blood pressure rising. A terrible time to have such an explosive conversation. Realizing this, I turn my back to her.

"Pull!" I shout. No disc comes out. I wait a moment and yell again. "Pull!"

A clay pigeon shoots out and I immediately strike it. I watch with enjoyment as it explodes in the air. I turn around, the barrel of the shotgun facing my mother-in-law. I watch her expression. For a moment, her face changes to fear, until I lower the barrel to the ground.

"I think you've overstayed your welcome," I say to

her. "I don't care who you sleep with, but when you do it in my house, you put me in a weird position. I think you get that somewhere in your thick skull. I've had enough of your fake pleasantries. I want you to leave my home."

After a moment, Delores smiles at me. "I must say, I like this side of you. I didn't think you had any... what do the men call it? Balls. I thought I could blow and push you over, dear. I thought you would leave. I wanted to show my son the real you, like I see you. I also see you're willing to fight." She reaches into her purse. For a moment my heart races, wondering if she has more shotgun shells in it. She pulls out a cigarette and lights it.

I turn my back to her and point the barrel of the shotgun to the sky again. "Pull!" I yell confidently.

CHAPTER 29

Delores speeds back home. The whole ride is awkwardly quiet. She parks in the driveway but doesn't take off her seatbelt.

"Tell my son I say hello," she says, looking out the windshield.

I take the hint and get out of the vehicle. After I close the door, she puts her car in gear, turns the vehicle back toward the front gate, and speeds off. I watch as her car leaves, wondering where she's going now. Part of me is happy it's not inside my house though. After the encounter at the gun range, I'll be fine never talking to my darling mother-in-law again. I will jump for joy when I see the moving truck take all of her crap out of my house. I will gleefully help Hannah pack all the boxes of Delores's belongings so she can leave and never come back.

I don't see any visits in the near future with my mother-in-law.

I also don't see any more special outings with her. Just when I thought going out with Delores couldn't get any worse, it does. This time I was briefly scared for my life.

The way she pointed the shotgun at me at the range will be etched in my mind forever. She knows all about gun safety. Despite that, she pointed a gun at me. It didn't matter that it was empty – the message was clear.

Then again, I pointed a loaded shotgun at her as well. Hopefully my message was clear.

This is my home, not hers. Her son is my husband. I'm not going anywhere. She, on the other hand, will be leaving very soon.

The front door of my home opens and Cero walks out, mumbling something under his breath. He stops in front of me and says something in Spanish. I don't speak a word of his language, but I can tell from his demeanour that whatever he said wasn't very nice. I watch him as he gets into his beat-up car and drives away.

Part of me wonders if he's driving to catch up with Delores.

I walk inside my home and Leo is standing in the living room, his hand on his head as if he has a terrible headache.

"Is everything okay?" I ask.

"Why didn't you tell me?" he says looking up at me. He knows, I realize. I can see Hannah in the kitchen, who glances at me quickly before she continues to clean the stove. "Let's go to our room." Leo waves at me to follow him.

Once we're inside, I immediately apologize to him, knowing exactly where this conversation is going.

"How long have you known?" he asks.

"I walked in on them the other day. That's why I stayed at my mother's house. I couldn't come back home."

"I just feel betrayed... by everyone. I mean, Cero? How long have they been— together?" His face sours at his own words.

I take a deep breath, remembering what Delores said at the gun range. "I think it's been for a while." He sighs. "Was it Charles that told you?"

He nods. "He waited a full day to tell me what happened." He laughs. "He hoped you'd be the one to break the news. Today when I went into the office and I still had no clue, he felt compelled to tell me."

"I wanted to tell you too," I say. "I didn't want to say anything over the phone."

He nods again. "I don't even know what to think right now. I wish I could do more than fire that piece of shit." He clenches his fist. "I told him if I saw him again..." He lowers his head. "What was my mom thinking?" He looks at me. "Did I see you get out of my mom's car?"

"Yeah. She took me to the Foothills Firearm Center," I say, raising my eyebrows.

He looks at me, confused. "I don't understand."

"She warned me not to get involved in her business," I tell him. I'm about to tell him how she aimed a weapon at me when she said it, but I think about my own response and don't.

He scoffs. "And she left just now. Did she say where?" I shake my head. "Oh, god. She's probably with him now. I didn't think she was that kind of woman. I mean, I didn't get along with my dad, but she was having an affair? I don't even know what to think." He looks at me. "I think I'm going to go back to the office."

"No, it's okay. Stay."

He shakes his head. "I don't think I want to be in this house right now." It's a feeling I completely understand. "I'll be back later tonight." He opens the bedroom door, and I walk him to the front door. "I'll be okay," he says calmly. "I just need to think about all of this. It's a lot." He kisses my forehead before leaving.

As I watch him enter his vehicle, Hannah steps up behind me. "We need to talk. I found something."

CHAPTER 30

Hannah pulls me into the kitchen to talk.

"What's wrong?" I ask.

"I couldn't help myself," she says. "I've been putting away that old hag's boxes and one of them contained some legal documents."

"You snooped in my mother-in-law's room?"

She shakes her head. "More like I was putting stuff away and couldn't help but notice."

I sigh. "Well, what did you find?"

She raises an eyebrow. "Something very interesting. The will of Leonard Sterling, or the original will. He changed it a month before his death."

"He just changed it?"

"That's right. Originally, everything he had was going to go to your mother-in-law. The will had been in place for over twenty years. Then suddenly he had a change of heart. A list of charities was given everything. He wrote his own wife out of his will. And then he added Leo to it as well. Only the thousand dollars to him, though," she says, confused. "Nothing compared to the amount those charities received."

"Leo told me about that. It was a spiteful inheritance," I say making a face.

She shakes her head. "Rich people drama. You give me

money when you die, and I'll be happy."

"These aren't normal people," I say, and Hannah agrees. Finally, it hits me why a man would change his will suddenly. "My father-in-law must have known about the affair with Cero."

"Bingo," Hannah says with a smile. "I feel like I'm pretty good at this sleuthing. The question is, what do we do about it?"

"We?" I repeat. I remind myself what Leo told me. "The insurance company cut her a check and it's coming any day now. Leo promised me he'd get her set up out of the house soon. Let's just let this be."

"Let it be? I mean, this is potentially murder we're talking about. Delores thought she was going to get every penny from her husband, and after she and her lover did the deed, she realized the truth. She got nothing."

I lower my head. Did Tony Cardone know about the change in the will? He must have. The lawyers would have to tell him who gets the life insurance, but that would have been at the burial of Leonard Sterling. Did Tony have access to the will before the funeral?

Part of me is curious and wants to call him. I remind myself of how my last conversation went with him, though. I also think of my husband.

"I won't do anything without Leo," I say. "This is his mother. I won't go behind his back to do some pseudo-investigation."

"Well, meanwhile there's plenty more boxes your mother-in-law has. Who knows what other information could be found."

I shake my head. "Do yourself a favor. Don't get involved any more than you have already. This is a mess you don't want to get into... I wish I never was. You should just go home. Take a few days off. Maybe she'll be packing up soon enough and we won't have to deal with any of this. Go ahead," I say. "Go home early."

"And leave you alone in this house? I don't think so. I'll leave when Leo comes back."

CHAPTER 31

Leo came home late and Hannah, to her word, left after he arrived.

Leo wasn't up for talking much and I didn't blame him. We went to bed almost immediately. Despite being in my fertile days, there was nothing happening in our bedroom. I'm sure neither of us were exactly in the mood for it.

Before going to sleep, Leo told me he loved me. That was enough for me to sleep that night even though I wanted to talk it out with him more.

In the morning, Leo brushes his teeth while I sprawl out in our bed. All I want to do is talk to my husband, but he has to work. To my surprise, he pops his head out of the bathroom, a thin smile on his face.

"I'm taking today off," he says.

"Really?"

"I probably shouldn't, and Charles's anxiety will go into overdrive, but I need a day to myself."

"Okay, no problem," I say. I lay back down in the bed. Give him space. He needs it right now.

"Well, not by myself. I was hoping we could go on a date?" he says shyly. "It's been a while since we went out, just the two of us. I thought it would be nice. What do you say?"

"A day date with my husband? I love that! What were you thinking?"

"That's my surprise," he says with a wide smile. "I just need a shower and we can go when you're ready."

"Perfect," I say. "Did... your mother come home?"

He shakes his head. "I went out to get some coffee in the kitchen. I knocked on her door but she's not there. I don't see her car either."

"She's okay," I tell him.

"I'd like a day where we just don't think about her, okay?"

I nod instead of screaming *yes*! I'm happy that he wants the same. Let's pretend she doesn't live with us and just enjoy our day together. *Perfect.*

I remember the talk I had with Hannah last night. I wonder how much Leo knows about his father's will. I wonder what thoughts are in his head right now. Does he suspect Cero or his mother being involved in his father's death?

I remind myself that there's a reason why the police aren't knocking down our door looking for Delores. There's still a lack of proof. A last-minute change of a will because of an affair doesn't mean anything. Perhaps there is some motive, but even if there was, it doesn't mean Delores did anything.

Despite Hannah's sudden interest in what happened, all signs still point to suicide.

Leo heads into the bathroom and turns on the shower. I get ready for the day as I listen to my husband whistling. Leo always has such a positive energy, even when things are tough... and they are. His father killed himself. His mother moved in and is driving us both mad. He finds out about her affair. He tells me his business is doing well, but I know better. There's a reason he's been so busy lately having late meetings. It's not for fun.

Times are tough.

Despite that, he's taking a day for himself to have fun with his wife, and that's why I love my husband. I'm his stress reliever. Spending time with me makes everything better. That puts a smile on my face because I feel the same. I love being around him and spending time together.

I wonder what he has planned for us today. I read some of my new books for a while as I wait for Leo to get ready. For a change my husband won't be going to work or staying in his home office all day. We'll be out together, and I want to have fun.

DPI.

I can almost hear the term in my head as if Tony Cardone is saying them. Dots per inch. The suicide note was not printed at my father-in-law's house or his office. Besides his home and office, where else did Leonard Sterling go?

I try to get the investigator out of my head. I try not to think of them, but the letters are haunting me.

Leo continues to whistle in the shower. I get out of bed and open the hallway door quietly. Down the hall, I see Hannah walking into the living room. She's here early. I wonder how much of that is because she's worried what will happen when Leo leaves the house and if Delores comes home. Or perhaps she wants to get in some early snooping. She seemed a little too excitable playing detective last night.

I walk down the hallway to one of the rooms closest to mine, opening the door. I turn on the light in Leo's office. It illuminates the room and all the funny knick knacks he has on his desk. For an adult, he enjoys childish things.

There's a comic framed on the wall. A first edition of some type of Spider-Man comic. I'm sure it cost a lot no matter how silly it seems to me. He even made his own bobble head that looks like him. He told me he bought one that looked like Charles and gifted it to him last Christmas.

Leo thought it was hilarious. Knowing how serious Charles is, I bet he was indifferent.

I walk around to the front of the desk and look at the paperwork that's scattered across it. If I wasn't sneaking around, I'd want to organize it for my husband. How can he work in such a mess? You wouldn't think a high earner would work at a station like this.

Behind the desk on a small table is his printer. I stand beside it. Guilt strikes me. I feel like I'm snooping on his phone or breaching his privacy somehow. It's silly, really. It's a printer, not anything personal.

Why am I even looking at it? I think about leaving my husband's office, but the urge to know the specifics of his printer quality overwhelms me. I examine it, looking for some kind of symbol or writing. I need to know what its DPI is. Unfortunately, I'm not tech savvy. I don't even remember the last time I used a printer. I look around the front but can't find any identifiers.

I pick it up and look underneath. Twenty-four hundred DPI.

I smile. This printer has a higher DPI than the printed suicide note.

It hits me. Delores has her own office. She set it up a few days ago with the help of movers. Could she have a printer? I look outside the window and don't see Delores's car.

"What are you doing?" I turn and Leo is looking at me, a thin smile on his face. "What are you doing with my printer?" He laughs.

I put it down on the table and laugh as well. "I wanted to print off some pictures of us. I was checking to see the quality of your printer... You have a good one." I smile back.

He raises his eyebrows at me. "Okay, well, that's good, I guess. Ready to go?"

CHAPTER 32

I continue getting ready for my day date with Leo, wondering what my husband is thinking of me right now. He caught me in his office. He doesn't know what I was looking for, but I never go in there.

Now I have to actually print pictures of us, since I backed myself into a corner with that excuse.

DPI. Stupid Tony Cardone. I wish he never told me the term. I'm going nuts sneaking around looking at people's printers. How many more printers do I need to see? Just one, I suppose. If my mother-in-law has poor print quality, what does that mean? Am I really going to suspect someone of murder because of a printer?

The whole thing is stupid. Silly! And yet I can't stop thinking about it.

When I walk into the hallway, I see Leo talking to Hannah. I take the opportunity to sneak to Delores's side of the house. I attempt to open the second door where I believe her office is, but it won't budge.

She locked it?

Why am I not surprised? It's my house and my mother-in-law is locking doors to rooms that don't belong to her.

Leo walks into the foyer and smiles at me. "Good to go," he says. I nod. "I gave Hannah the day off again. It's been tense here. Everything with my mom has just made things hard. I don't want her to be home when she comes back. I know how my mom is."

I smile. "Good idea," I say. I wanted the same. Hannah needs to be away from my house. "I just want to say hi to her before we leave."

Leo goes out to his vehicle. When he's out of sight, I walk into the kitchen and greet Hannah.

"A day date," she says with a smile. "That's nice."

"Are you leaving soon? Leo gave you the day off. You should go before Delores comes back."

"I'm just finishing cleaning a few things and I'll lock up. Don't worry. Go have fun."

I sigh. "You plan on snooping again, don't you?"

She shrugs. "I can't help myself at this point. Rich people have mysteries and I have to solve them."

I sigh again. "Listen, don't stay long." I turn to leave but look back at her. "But if you do snoop, try and see if she has a printer and check the DPI of it. Her office door is locked so it could be in there. Then go home!"

CHAPTER 33

Leo drives into downtown Calgary and parks near a trail we used to take often. Princess Island Park. It's located in the middle of downtown with tall buildings surrounding it, but the park is majestic. To get to the park you have to cross a bridge. In the spring and summer, all the geese raise their goslings. We would come and watch the families grow. There's easily hundreds of birds in this small area.

There's not nearly as many here today, though. Only a few goslings with their mama and papa. The park is still beautiful and brings back wonderful memories I've had with Leo.

"I love this place," I say to him with a smile. He nods.

"I loved taking you here too. I miss coming here with you when we lived nearby. Now that we're so far away, I have to admit that I miss it." He wraps his arm around me as we walk.

I nestle my head in his shoulder. "So, what else do you have planned today?" I ask eagerly. "Any more surprises?"

He smiles. "Well, coffee at our favorite place nearby. Lunch somewhere else. Maybe a movie?"

I smile back. Not exactly the most romantic idea for a day date, but time with my husband, especially away from his mother, is time well spent. I'm already having so much fun being with him. He's starting to run out of terrible jokes to share with me as we walk up to the small bridge, and he starts to slow down.

I match his pace. "What?" I ask.

He stops completely and looks around. "Yep, I think it was this spot exactly."

I laugh. "What are you talking about?"

"You really don't remember, do you?" He gives a thin smile. "You know, I think men are truly more romantic than women. We're the ones who do all the romantic things."

I laugh when it hits me. "I remember. Very romantic."

He nods. "In this exact spot is where I told you I loved you for the first time. I can still remember it like it was yesterday. We were surrounded by all the geese and their goslings. Their sounds and the rest of nature was captivating against the backdrop of the downtown high-rise buildings. Despite the beauty around me, all I could think about was your beauty. How much I loved you, and I had to say it for the first time." I kiss him, and we both laugh, kissing again. "The first of many, many times."

"This is the best date ever," I say, holding him close.

We reminisce some more over coffee at a nearby cafe. It's the same one we went to after he told me he loved me. The restaurant we go to was also the same one we went to that day. I'm beginning to see the theme he had in mind. While we can't watch the same movie we had several years ago, we still go to the theatre. The movie's terrible, but I don't care. He holds me and whispers into my ear the entire time.

I feel just as much in love with my husband as I did the day he told me he loved me.

On the way home, we laugh more as we reminisce

about when we dated. I hope that Delores won't be home, because I have only one thing in mind to do with Leo when we get back. As we park outside the house, I'm upset to see her car. That won't stop me from continuing to have the perfect day date with my husband.

We laugh as we walk up the steps and open the front door. When Leo steps inside he lets go of me instantly, his mouth wide open in shock.

I peer inside and take a step in. Delores is standing near the staircase. Below her is the twisted body of Hannah at the foot of the stairs.

CHAPTER 34

I stay in my bedroom while the authorities remove the body of my friend from the bottom of the stairs.

I've spoken to several officers, going over the same story. I tell them everything. I don't hold back.

I know in my heart Delores has something to do with Hannah's death. Just as Tony Cardone suspects my father-in-law's death wasn't suicide, I know Hannah's death wasn't an accident.

Despite that, one of the officers I speak to called it just that. A terrible freak accident. A young woman didn't pay attention as she walked down a spiral staircase and fell to her death. A box belonging to Delores was beside her body.

I can't get the image of Delores beside Hannah out of my mind. It was as if she wanted me to walk in and see my friend's lifeless body myself. She wanted me to see her beside my friend. Make sure I knew it was her.

My mind may be playing tricks on me, but in my head, I picture Delores smiling at me as I look at Hannah. I cringe at the thought of seeing my friend's twisted body, her head twisted in an unnatural direction.

Her death would have been quick, one of the policemen told me. That doesn't matter. Her death was not an accident. What actually matters is it was murder, and the murderer is living in my house.

I told the police the same story. I told them everything I could. I told them about my father-in-law's suspicious death. The affair. I even told them about the shooting range. One of the officers I spoke to asked if I wanted to press charges against Delores. Given that I pointed a loaded gun back at her, I declined. I also failed to tell the officer that part of the story. I'd be the one getting arrested, not her, if I had.

After speaking to the officers in my bedroom, they left. Outside, Leo and Delores were speaking to the police as well. I wonder what they are saying now.

I can imagine Delores. "Poor girl. She wasn't watching where she was going."

Delores didn't call the police until after our arrival. She stated that she just got back home herself and found Hannah at the bottom of the stairs. When asked why she didn't call the police right away, Delores said she was in a state of shock.

She told the police that she had an alibi for where she was. Of course it was with Cero.

I listened to what she said to the police and wanted to interject, telling them what I knew. I was surprised they were even talking to the police to begin with.

Never talk to the authorities, the Sterlings told me. Despite that, they're both being interviewed by the police individually now and answering their questions.

An image of Hannah's twisted head hits my imagination again.

Why didn't she leave? Leo told her to leave. I told her to leave... only I didn't. I encouraged her to look for more evidence. Hannah wanted to learn more about Leonard Sterling's death, and now she's dead.

A terrible accident.

A few hours ago, we were laughing. Last night she stayed with me to console me. Make sure I was safe. Now, she'll be buried just like Leonard Sterling.

The two have something in common. Their murderer. Nobody will believe me though. Except maybe one person.

I take out my cell phone and dial his number.

He answers immediately. "Cardone."

"I have things I need to tell you," I say.

CHAPTER 35

"Are you sure you don't want to wait for your lawyers, Mrs. Sterling?" he says playfully.

"I'm serious this time."

"I'm surprised to hear from you again, Mrs. Sterling." I can imagine the look on his smug face. "Please know that I won't stay on the phone for more abuse."

I ignore his comments. "She killed again."

"Who?"

"Delores Sterling. She murdered my friend, Hannah. My husband and I hired my friend to be our housemaid. Today she was found at the bottom of our staircase, dead. The police are still at my house."

"Why don't you tell them your thoughts?" he says.

"I did. They don't believe me."

He sighs. "It's frustrating, isn't it? When you know something is wrong but can't prove it. You know, how I've felt since Leonard Sterling's murder."

"I believe you now," I say, breathing heavily into the phone. "What can we do about it? How do we prove it?"

"First, tell me what you know. You've been holding out on me, haven't you?"

I take a deep breath. "Delores has been having an affair with her landscaper. His name is Cero Rivero. I think they've been keeping it a secret for some time."

There's a pause before Tony speaks. "I already know that."

"You know?"

"I followed Delores after her husband died. I discovered that some time ago. They met at hotels in downtown Calgary after the suicide. When I told my company, it certainly raised some eyebrows, but in the end they didn't care. People having affairs doesn't usually end with murder. I was told I needed more."

I take a deep breath again. "Well, the other day, my friend Hannah found documents that showed Leonard Sterling changed his will right before his death so that all his money went to charity. I suspect he discovered the affair and changed what his wife was to receive."

This time Tony sighs. "I knew that too. I was hoping you'd have more than this. I'm truly disappointed."

I shake my head as if he's in the room with me. "My friend is dead. They removed her body from my house tonight. I don't like how you're talking to me."

There's a pause before he continues. "I'm sorry. I am. I wish we could have caught her before she killed again."

"What do you know about Cero Rivera?" I ask. "He has to be involved more in this."

"Not much. Some of your in-laws' other staff said that he's from Ontario."

I nod. "I knew that, but that's all I know. Can you look into his background more?"

"I've tried. He's not on social media and I can't find any more information on him."

I sigh. "Tony, can't you look into him more professionally than what a Google search can provide?"

"I'll look into it," he says sharply.

I think about Tony's determination to prove his

theories about Leonard Sterling's death. It truly goes above and beyond what most workers would do. "What's in this for you?" I ask.

"What do you mean?"

"The police have already closed the case. Your company has issued a check to Delores Sterling. Everything is done. Why do you still care?"

There's another long pause before he answers. "A promotion," he says.

I cover my head. "You have to be kidding me. Everything you've done was for a promotion?"

"You wanted me to be honest with you. I am. There's a big one available. Head of claims. If I'm able to show that the death of Leonard Sterling was committed by the wife, the company will take back the money we issued. I'll have saved the company over a million dollars. For that, I can write my ticket to any position in this company I want. Head of claims or even higher. Or any other company I want to work for, for that matter."

"Unbelievable," I say. I can feel my blood pressure rising.

"Despite my intentions, you know I'm telling the truth. Leonard Sterling did not kill himself. He was murdered. Your friend, now dead, may she rest in peace, did not die from an accident. They are connected. You know it. Now you have to prove it."

"How? You know I actually checked my husband's printer for its print quality today?"

"And?"

"He has a high-quality printer. My mother-in-law has an office in our home, though. I think she may have a printer."

"Check it out," he says.

"The door is locked. I didn't even know there was a lock on the door. There has to be another way to prove Delores murdered two people."

"Wear a wire," Tony says. "Try and get her to confess."

I scoff at the idea. "Tony, what the hell are you talking about? Are you just saying whatever comes to your head for ideas? This is useless. You are useless."

"Well, I don't hear any ideas coming from you," he says.

"What can I do? I have a two-time murderer living in my house."

"I'm not sure," he says coldly. "But stay safe."

CHAPTER 36

Leo walks into the bedroom as I hang up on Tony.
"Who's that?" he asks.
I take a deep breath. "I can't stay here anymore."
"It's terrible what happened to your friend, Madelyn, I know, but this is still our home."
"I wish we never moved here," I say, fighting back the tears. "Ever since we did, my whole life has been chaos. Ever since your mother moved in."
Leo shakes his head. "She's going to be leaving soon. I told you. Don't worry."
"I am worried!" I yell. "She killed Hannah."
Leo lets out a puff of air and shakes his head. "What? No. Stop saying stuff like that."
"She pushed her down the stairs! Made it look like an accident after." An image of Hannah's twisted body at the bottom of the stairs hits me again. I know it will give me nightmares for years to come.
"Stop, Madelyn! You're working yourself up. I saw her almost trip down the stairs last week. Those steps are a hazard. We're going to remodel this house eventually. Remove those stupid stairs."
"I can't live here while your mother stays."
Leo takes a deep breath. "Why would my mom kill Hannah? You're not making any sense. You're upset.

Angry. Your friend died. Blaming my mom won't change anything. It was a terrible—"

"Accident?" I yell back. "It wasn't. Hannah was going through your mom's things, looking for more evidence."

"Evidence of what?" Leo says, confused.

"It was your mom who murdered your father!"

Leo scoffs and shakes his head again. "What are you talking about? Now my mother murdered two people. Her husband? The maid?"

"She killed Hannah because she found evidence. The affair with Cero was going on for some time. You know that part. Did you know that your father changed his will a month before his death? He totally removed your mother from it! He added in a small amount for you out of spite. To get back at you for taking your mother's side. Now you're doing the same. Don't take her side over mine now!"

Leo lowers his head. "I'm not taking sides. I never have. I married you. We are together. My side is with you, but I can't sit here and listen to what you're saying. My father discovered the affair and changed his will? That doesn't mean my mom would kill him for it, if she even knew about it."

I sigh. "She killed Hannah. She was going to look into your mother's office at her printer. She was going to check the DPI. Delores must have caught her."

"DPI?" Leo repeats. "What the hell are you talking about now?"

I sigh. "Dots per inch. I spoke to that investigator, Tony Cardone. Your father's suicide note was printed on a printer with a low DPI, but none of the printers in his house or his office match. That means the note was printed somewhere else. Your mother has an office. She must have a printer! Hannah was snooping. She must have been caught and next thing you know, killed for what she found."

Laughter erupts in the hallway as Delores comes into my bedroom. "Are you seriously calling me a murderer because of printer ink? Next time I murder someone, will I leave a trail of post-it notes for you to follow?" She looks at Leo. "Son, this is ridiculous! She's delusional! How can you listen to any of this?"

"You threatened me the other day to not get involved in your business. Hannah did, and now I see you meant what you said!"

"Threatened you?" Delores says. She looks at Leo, who seems dumbfounded by the entire conversation.

I take a step towards her, my pointer finger emphasising my words. "You pointed a gun at me and threatened me not to get involved!"

She laughs again. "Darling, the gun was empty. Do you really think I would point a loaded weapon at you? I'm not a psycho! I was upset that I thought you told my son about Cero, and when I turned to confront you on it, I momentarily forgot about the gun. It wasn't loaded." She looks at her son. "It was poor of me, but not on purpose. She, however, is very much a psycho. She pointed a loaded gun at me on purpose and threatened me! She demanded that I leave her home, or else."

Leo looks at me and I can see anger in his eyes. I've never seen such a look from my husband, and for a moment, I feel intimidated. Delores for a change is telling the truth and I know it looks bad.

"You did what?" Leo shouts. "You pointed a shotgun at my mother?"

I take a deep breath. "I did. I felt threatened. I was

scared!" Leo turns away from me. "I wasn't going to do anything. I just want her to know I wasn't scared of her."

"By pointing a gun at her," Leo says, covering his face.

"She killed Hannah!" I repeat. "She murdered your father. I cannot stay in this house any longer with her because I know who's next."

Delores shakes her head. "You're delusional, darling. You need medication."

"Shut up!" I shout. Leo puts his hand up, attempting to calm the situation, but failing miserably.

"I don't even own a printer, dear," Delores says, shaking her head. "You're foolish. You've accused me of killing my husband!"

"Who you probably hated!" I yell. "You have Cero to comfort you now. He probably helped you with everything!"

Leo looks at me sternly. "Enough!"

I take a step back. "Tell her to open her office door. She locked it. Tell her to open it and we can see if she has a printer. We can see the DPI."

She laughs. "This is ridiculous! Now Cero is a murderer as well? What are you playing? Clue, darling? Cero, in my office, with a poor-quality printer?"

Leo lowers his head. "Just open the door, Mother. Let her see."

She looks at her son. "You're truly giving this thought? After everything I've done for you? I've given my life to ensure you had everything you needed, and you turn around and accuse me of the ultimate sin? I gave birth to you. How could you do this to me? Your wife needs professional help, dear. I've been nothing but nice to her and look what she does!"

"Stop gaslighting him!" I yell. "Open your office door

like he said."

She scoffs and looks at her son. Leo nods. "The door, Mom. Just open it."

"Fine," Delores shouts and storms down the hallway. I quickly follow her to make sure she doesn't hide anything at the last minute. She goes into her bedroom and comes out with a key and opens the neighboring door. "There you go, dear," she says. "Find your smoking gun. Or DPM or whatever you called it."

Delores shakes her head as she watches me enter her office. Leo stands behind his mother and does the same.

I enter the room slowly. I see no printer on the desk or anywhere else in the room. "It must be in one of her boxes," I say.

She laughs and looks at her son. "I don't have a printer, dear. I never have. Why would I need one?"

"Why do you need an office?" I ask.

She takes a deep breath. "When you're a stay-at-home mother, you try your best to find meaning. I liked organizing group dates for the girls' club or other activities I do. I like to have a space that's just mine. I never thought this would incriminate me for murder!" She begins to tear up, and my mouth drops when I see Leo console her. "I mean, your father was a difficult man to love. What I did was wrong with Cero. All I wanted was to feel love, son. That's all. You left our home. You barely talked to me after you got married."

He sighs. "That wasn't because of you, or because of Madelyn," he says. "The fight with Dad was bad, Mom. I couldn't go back."

"All I wanted was love," Delores repeats and cries into her son's shoulder. The sight makes me sick. I look around the room and open a box near me.

"Madelyn," Leo says. "That's enough."

"It's here somewhere," I say, searching through the contents.

"You looked in my office today too," Leo says. I stop rummaging in the box and stand up, looking guiltily at my husband. "You checked the quality of my printer. You weren't planning on printing pictures of us on it. You were trying to see if my printer matched the one you feel the suicide note was printed from, right?"

"Leo," I plead in a soft voice.

He shakes his head and lets go of his mother. "No. I'm right. That investigator got in your head, and you thought I…" He takes a deep breath. "I can't believe we're having this discussion."

"Leo." I look over at Delores, who gives me a thin smile. I feel rage building inside me. "I can't stay in this house with her," I say, pointing at his mother.

"I think you need to leave," Leo says. He clears his throat. "No, you need to leave."

CHAPTER 37

I stay at a hotel downtown. I thought about driving several hours to be with my mom, but it would have been too long of a drive. Since arriving in my room, I've managed to plop myself on the queen bed and do nothing except think of all the terrible events that have happened.

I've been kicked out of my own home and it's all because of my mother-in-law.

I shouldn't have been so explosive with what I said to Leo though. I gave Delores so much ammunition to use against me tonight. Part of me wonders if I'll ever be able to return to my house, or to my husband.

My mother-in-law has successfully ruined my life. I'm not sure if that was her intention when she moved in. Nothing the woman does makes sense to me.

The face Leo had when his mother told him I pointed a loaded shotgun at her was enough to know I lost the battle immediately. How could he trust me?

I don't understand how he can trust her.

Of course, it's because Delores knows how to manipulate her son. Leo took the bait. I've been kicked out. My marriage is already peaking after a year together. Delores must be thrilled.

Everything in my life has erupted at once. It's overwhelming. I'm not sure whether to scream into my pillow or dry my tears on it. I've done both since checking in.

I look through the large hotel window that faces downtown. From up high, I can hear the muffled sound of the city below. I'm not used to it anymore. It's quiet on our acreage. I can spot my neighbors' home in the distance.

Here though, everything and everyone is crammed together downtown.

I look out into the distance, wondering if I can somehow manage to see the area where my house is, but of course I can't. I wonder what happened after I left. Leo and his mother were shouting at each other as I stormed out. I didn't even bother grabbing anything to go to the hotel with.

I just wanted to leave.

How are we ever going to get over this? I think of Hannah and clench my fist. I'm not sure I can ever be around my mother-in-law again.

I've thought about calling the police. One of the detectives gave me their card. I'm not sure what I'd say to them beyond what I already have. I'd continue to point the finger at my mother-in-law, and they'd continue to look away.

At her age, how could she murder two people?

They don't care about the changes to my father-in-law's will or the affair Delores had. They definitely do not care about my fixation on printers. I cover my head. I must have looked hysterical to Leo, raving about printer ink.

All I know is Hannah didn't die in an accident. She was murdered. I'll do whatever I have to to prove it.

I look at the clock beside the bed. It's nearly midnight. I haven't been able to relax since I arrived. I've tried putting on the television to take my mind off things, but it doesn't work. All I can think about is Hannah or the look Delores had on her face as I got kicked out of my own house.

I sit on the edge of bed and fall backwards. I feel defeated.

She's won.

My phone buzzes in my jeans pocket. I take it out and my expression changes when I see it's Leo.

"Hey," I say, answering the call.

"I'm glad you're awake," he says in a hushed voice. "I was worried you went to bed. I can't sleep."

"Me neither."

"I…" He sighs and takes a long pause before continuing. "I don't know what to even say."

"Me neither," I say again.

"That was really intense," he says. "I never thought—I don't even know what to think."

I take a deep breath. "I keep thinking of Hannah."

"I know," he says. "I think of her too. You two were close. I want to be there for you, but I can't right now. I'm really upset. I'm upset with both of you."

I lower my head. "I'm sorry. I wish things were different. It's better that I left. I can't be there with her right now."

"She says the same. She won't stay here with you either, she tells me, but I need you to come back. I need you to come home to me. I can't live like this forever. You're my wife."

Tears are forming, and I can't stop them from rolling down the side of my face into the hotel comforter. "So she won't leave, and I won't come back."

"That's the situation," he says. "At least for now. I told

her that she does need to leave, though, and as soon as possible."

"You did?" I feel a smile spreading across my face.

"You're my wife," he says. "I want to share this house with you. She needs to leave. I know that, and now she does. We fought a lot after you left. I'm giving her a few days. I'll help put her up in a hotel somewhere. I told her if she wants help figuring out what to do next, I'll be there, but she needs to leave."

My smile widens. I want to shout in excitement. Suddenly his tone changes.

"We have a lot to talk about, though," he says. "What happened tonight changes everything. There's no coming back from accusations like what you said."

I lower my head again. "I know... Are we okay, though?"

He pauses. "Why did you sneak into my office? You really thought I was involved?" I don't answer. "I'm not sure how to feel right now, Madelyn. I don't. This is all just too much. We have a lot to talk about, but I don't want to do it over the phone. It's best that you don't come back home until she leaves. I'll tell you when she does, and you can come back. We can talk then… Where are you now?"

"A hotel, downtown," I say, trying to not let the severity of his words hit me.

"I'm going to be working a lot the next few days, and it's probably for the best. I won't call you for a while. I just need time myself to think about everything."

His words sink in my chest. "Do you need a break from me?"

"I do," he admits. "I'll talk to you soon."

I cover my face, wiping the tears. "Okay. Goodnight."

There's a long pause before he speaks. "I still love

you."

CHAPTER 38

The hotel allowed a late check out. I took my time getting ready. I've texted and called my mom but so far she hasn't called or messaged back. I didn't want to text her what happened. All I asked is if she could call me when she can. I know my mom will be okay if I come back to her house for a few days.

This time I'll tell her everything. After what Leo said to me last night, it feels like our marriage is forever changed because of what happened. Everything is different, he said. I feel it too, and I'm scared about what that means.

My cell rings and I immediately pick it up. "Hey, Mom," I say.

"No, it's Cardone," the investigator says with his usual harsh tone.

"Oh, great. It's you," I say. I can't tell if meeting Tony Cardone made everything worse for me or better. Since he knocked on my front door, my life has changed for the worse. I'm not sure who I hate more at this exact moment, Tony or my mother-in-law.

"Where are you?" he asks. "Are you at home?"

"No, I actually got kicked out by my husband and mother-in-law. I accused Delores Sterling of murdering my friend and her husband, and Leo kicked me out." I laugh. I think about the conversation I had with Leo last night. "I'm not sure where things are in my marriage right now."

"I'm sorry to hear that. I am," he says, softening his tone. "But I'm glad you're out of that house. I found out some things."

"What now?" I ask.

"Cero Rivera. That's not his real name."

My mouth drops as he says it. "What do you mean?"

"I told you I couldn't find much information on him. You made fun of me for that, but I hired a private investigator who couldn't find much history either, but he did find a lot about a man named Marco Rivarios. Same birthday, and the picture on both driver's licenses are nearly identical. You told me Cero moved to Alberta from Ontario. Cero changed his name a few years ago before moving to Calgary. The name change likely had something to do with the three years he did in prison. Do you want to know what his convictions were for?"

"Murder?"

"Not at that time, no. Back then, fraud was his game. Mostly credit card fraud. Stealing information from the elderly to steal from them. When Cero moved to Calgary, he started working under the table for some landscaping company. Your father-in-law hired him instead of wanting to continue to pay the company."

"So, you think Cero is up to his old habits?"

Cardone doesn't answer. "I did some more digging. Did you know your husband has his life insurance policy with us as well? Now, this is technically a breach of contract, but in the circumstances, I'm worried about you. Do you want to know who gets Leo's life insurance money if he suddenly dies?"

I breathe out. "His mother."

"It's split, right down to the penny," Cardone says. "You and your mother-in-law share everything, and it's a lot."

I take in a deep breath. "What do we do?"

"I'm going to call the police detective on your father-in-law's case and reveal what I found out. I'm not sure if they'll bite and reopen the case, but I think I can raise enough hell for them to at least ask a few more questions. You, though, I think you should just stay put. Don't go back home."

"What about Leo?" I say. Tensions are high right now and he's kicking Delores out. There's no telling what could happen if he's not at least aware of what Cardone told me.

"Call him," Tony says. "Tell him. If he wants to talk to me, he can."

"He won't," I say confidently. "He's been trained by his mother not to talk to people like you."

"Well, that could put him in danger now," Tony says. "Do what you can. Invite him to stay with you at the hotel maybe. Something."

"Is there a way to know where Cero is now?" I ask. "I haven't seen him since Leo fired him."

"I have no clue. My hope is that after I speak to the detective on your father-in-law's death, that they'll attempt to locate him. Ask Cero questions. Maybe your mother-in-law too."

I breathe out. "I take it back, Tony. You're not entirely useless. Sorry!"

CHAPTER 39

I call Leo's cell immediately, but of course he doesn't answer. I call again and leave a message.

He's out at meetings, I tell myself. He's working. I know he's busy. Despite the more rational side of me knowing I shouldn't jump to the worst case scenario, I do. I imagine Delores, the wicked smile she wore when she pointed her shotgun at me at the range. It didn't matter that the shotgun was empty. She knew what she was doing. There was no forgotten lesson in gun safety. She wanted to scare me.

I think of Hannah. I try my best to not remember the last image of her that my brain continuously injects into my memory.

What will Delores do if her son turns his back on her? How far will she and Cero, or Marco as he was once called, go?

I call my husband again, hoping that it's true that third time's the charm. It's not, though.

I look through my phone contacts for his office number instead and call again. It continues to ring for what feels like forever before my husband's voice comes on.

"You've reached Leo Sterling. Please leave a message and I'll return your call as soon as I can. If this is an emergency, you can call Charles Rayer at—" I scramble around the hotel and thankfully find a notepad and pen on the desk, jotting down the number.

I shake my head as I dial the number. Please, Charles, pick up. The phone begins to ring and I wait with anticipation to hear his voice, but of course I don't. The phone continues to ring until Charles requests for me to leave a message. I leave one.

"Hey Charles," I say, trying to not sound too worried. "Call me when you get this, please."

I take my things from the room and check out of the hotel, quickly making my way to my car in the parking lot across the street. Leo works in downtown Calgary as well. His office is not too far away. With any luck, I can just meet up with him there. Downtown Calgary is a mess of a place to park, though, especially midweek during the daytime. All the other business professionals struggle to find places to park, and so today I've become one of them. I've passed my husband's office building several times but can't find a spot for the life of me. I give up and finally stop in a no-parking zone.

I don't care anymore. The only thing I care about is finding Leo. I get out of my car and, once I get my bearings, make my way quickly to my husband's building. I push open the glass doors and a cool rush of air conditioned air hits me. The hum of activity fills the air as people bustle about, rushing to their destination. Once inside, I look for the directory hung beside the elevator, confirming he's on the eighth floor.

The button is already illuminated with a group of people waiting for one of the two elevators to open. I glance to my side and see the stairway. I'm in for a workout today. I take the stairs and begin regretting it once I get to the fifth floor. I'm down to a slow walk by the time I hit the eighth.

When I enter the eighth-floor hallway, the elevator opens up and several people, some I remember from the first floor, exit, briefcases in their hands. I roll my eyes as I try to figure out which way his office is. It's been a long time since I've met up with my husband at his job.

Finally, I find the office door and I'm immediately disappointed when I see it's shut and the lights inside are off. It's only Charles and Leo that work here. Since they are a small organization, they're waiting to grow their business before hiring more staff. How I wish that were not the case. I imagine how easy it could be for me to ask a receptionist where my husband is when it's an emergency had he hired one.

Taped to one of the windows is a handwritten note. On it is both Leo's and Charles's cell numbers. I had called Charles's number before but after checking it the number on the sign, I realize that I must have called his office number.

I dial the number and pray for an answer. It rings a few times and I'm about to give up when, to my surprise, someone does pick up.

Only they don't say anything.

"Charles?" I ask. "Are you there? Hello? I need to speak to Leo."

Suddenly I hear the sound of shouting as the line disconnects. Confused, I dial the number again but this time it goes straight to voicemail. I call a third time but with the same result.

I wait for the elevator, wondering what I just heard.

I walk back to where my car is parked on the street. I'm thankful that it hasn't been towed but saddened to see a white piece of paper flapping in the wind underneath my windshield wiper. A ticket. Of course I have one even though I haven't been away from my car for too long. I should be happy, I suppose. It could have been towed.

I get in my car and try again to call Charles and then my husband but neither answer.

Frustrated, I do the one thing I said I wouldn't do. I begin driving back home. It feels like it takes forever to arrive, even though it's less than twenty minutes. As I drive along the street heading to my house, I'm surprised to see a car parked on the side of the road, one I've seen many times.

It's Charles Rayer's car. Why is it parked so far away from my house if he's there?

I drive up to the gate and hit the button to open it. I wait patiently until it does and drive down the long driveway to the house. I know I shouldn't be here right now. Leo told me to stay away. Even Tony Cardone said the same.

As if my body is trying to plead with me to get away, I feel my stomach turn as I get closer to my house. It's as if I'm scared to be near my home now.

Leo's Escalade is parked outside but not his Lamborghini. Usually he takes his Escalade out with him and rarely the sports car. Is he home?

Charles is here, though. He must be. To my dismay, so is Delores. Her Rolls-Royce is parked beside Leo's. I slowly get out of my car and reluctantly go up the steps. When I approach my front door, I feel like I'm a stranger. I ring the doorbell and smile to myself when I remember it's not working.

I'm about to knock when I realize how silly it is to do so. This is my home. I take my key and open the door.

"Hello?" I call out as I close the door behind me.

I'm about to yell for Leo when I hear shouting from Delores's side of the house.

"No! Stop! Please don't—" My eyes widen and ears sting with the blast of a shotgun. As I cover my head, a body slides into the hallway.

Shocked, I know I'm too late.

I stare at the twitching body on the floor and realize it's not Leo. When Charles Rayer sees me, he attempts to crawl closer until he stops moving altogether.

I'm still paralyzed with fear when my mother-in-law leaves her bedroom, the shotgun in her hands. She turns her head and looks directly at me.

CHAPTER 40

"Madelyn!" Delores shouts.

I finally snap out of it and run into the living room. I can hear the footsteps of Delores behind me. I wait to hear another blast from her shotgun as I run but she hasn't fired at me yet. I know she's not far behind me, but I don't dare turn to look.

I hate myself for not running outside and right to my car. Then again, Delores is quick enough to pump a round into my vehicle as I attempt to speed away. If I ran into the grounds, I would have been an easier target for a skeet-shooting champion like Delores.

"Madelyn!" she shouts again. I run through the kitchen and realize she's too close for me to run out the back door. Instead, I run up the stairs that lead to the den upstairs. As I do, I dial 911 on my cell. I'm completely out of breath when the operator answers.

"911. What's your emergency?"

"My mother-in-law is trying to kill me!" I manage in between panicked breaths.

"Stop, dear!" Delores shouts, making her way up the stairs.

"Hold while I connect you," the operator says.

"No, wait!" I shout, but it's too late as I'm put on hold. I hear Delores making her way up the stairs. Each step she takes is closer to me. I shout in terror as I run across the den. The blinding midday light of the afternoon shines at me through the panoramic windows.

"Stop!" Delores shouts again.

"Leave me alone!" I yell back. I run faster, but as I do, my phone slips from my fingers and slides across the floor. I panic and I'm about to grab it when I see Delores at the top of the steps, the shotgun aimed towards the ceiling.

I continue to dart towards the spiral staircase. I rush down the steps, catching my foot once, nearly tripping. I think of Hannah. I wonder if she had a similar fate, falling down these stairs while being chased by Delores. I slow down but a shout from Delores catches my attention. I look up and as I do, I lose track of my feet, tripping and falling down the remaining steps.

When I hit the bottom, I worry I'm paralyzed from my injuries but quickly realize it's just the shock of my situation. I hurry to stand up but immediately feel pain in my right leg and collapse again to the floor.

"'You don't understand!" Delores says. I hear her as she makes her way down the staircase herself. With any luck, she'll trip and fall beside me but somehow I know that won't be her fate.

I crawl across to the living room and hide behind the new couch that the movers placed just a few days prior. It's large enough to hide me but I realize in fear that a trail of blood gives away my hiding place.

I look above me, and the picture of Delores and Leo is there, Delores's wicked smile taunting me.

My mother-in-law takes the last step from the spiraling staircase and onto the main floor. "I know you're here, Madelyn. Don't hide. We need to talk. I know you are the one who called Charles. Why? Tell me now!"

She slowly walks to the end of the couch and looks directly at me. The shotgun is firmly in her hands. "You're with them?" she repeats.

I put my hands up and plead. "No, please. Don't kill me."

Delores aims her shotgun, but to my surprise, it's not directed at me.

"What are you doing?" I turn and Leo is at the front door, his eyes locked on his mother.

CHAPTER 41

"Put it down," Leo pleads.

Delores lowers the gun slowly, her mouth wide open at her son's arrival. I attempt to crawl towards him, but my mother-in-law looks down at me and I stop in my tracks.

"I knew it couldn't be true," Delores says. She stares at her son. "I knew it." She laughs. "You wouldn't do that to me." A tear forms in her eye as she looks back down at me, her face becoming more sinister. "Charles lied!" she screams. She looks at me with her dead eyes. "That's why you called Charles?"

"Mom!" Leo shouts. "Just put the shotgun down and we can talk. Please."

She ignores him and continues to stare at me intensely, the barrel of her gun facing the floor, but with the look in her eye, it could easily be redirected at me. "You called Charles to see if he did it, didn't you?"

My mouth drops. "I called him looking for Leo. I couldn't find him. I was scared."

"You should be scared," she says.

Leo takes a step towards her, and Delores moves back. "Don't!" she says. "Let me do this for both of us. Charles said it was you, my darling son, who planned to kill me, but I know it wasn't. You would never! I know Charles was lying to protect Madelyn!"

"What is she talking about?" I yell.

She looks down at me. "Charles tried to kill me! He said it was Leo who told him to do it. He confessed to everything before I blew that weasel away."

"You did what?" Leo shouts. He looks to his side and sees his business partner, what's left of him, a pile of stained red on the marble floor. He covers his face in shock.

Delores looks at her son, surprised. "He tried to kill me. He said you planned this with him!" she shouts. "I know you would never… I knew the moment your wife called Charles that my son was not involved." She looks at me again and raises her shotgun, directing it at my head. "When you called Charles, it set off his ringtone on his cell. I found him standing above me while I slept, a pillow in his hand. I clocked him in the head with a picture frame beside my bed before he could do anything. I got my shotgun, and when I pointed it at that boy, he told me everything. At least, I thought he was telling the truth." She looks at me, her rage-filled eyes getting darker. "Charles said you had nothing to do with it, despite you calling him. He tried to cover for you, but then you showed up at this house. I knew he lied. I shot him immediately."

I look over at Leo, confused. He's still staring at the body of Charles but finally snaps out of it. "Mom, don't hurt her!"

She walks up to me slowly and points the shotgun directly into my chest. "Ever since she came into our lives, everything has been a nightmare for me. It's all her fault. It all ends now."

Leo runs towards her, and Delores raises the shotgun

at her son. As she's distracted, with everything I can muster, I stand up quickly and grab her arms, keeping the shotgun between us. She yells into my face as I scream in terror at hers. She's much older than me, and I shrug her off. She falls to the floor, and I point the gun at her now.

"Shoot her!" Leo screams. I look at my husband, confused, and when I glance down at Delores, she is staring at her son with the same expression.

"It was you!" she screams at him.

"She's got another gun on her!" Leo shouts. "The handgun. She must have it on her. Don't let her take it out." I lower the shotgun for a moment but when Delores shuffles on the floor, I immediately aim it back at her. "Shoot! Before she kills us both! Give me the gun. I'll take care of this."

He storms over to me, but before he can grab the gun, Delores shouts, "He's responsible for Hannah!"

I take a step back and stare at my husband.

"Don't listen to her," Leo says. "She's messing with you like she always does. Give me the gun to control this situation."

Delores laughs. "I didn't want to believe it when Charles told me the truth. Him and my son made an arrangement. Leo killed Charles's mother and father. He did something to their vehicle to make it crash. Even if police figured out what my son did to it, Charles had the perfect alibi. They wouldn't suspect Leo either. What reason could he have for killing Charles's parents?"

"Why would he do that?" I say.

Leo shakes his head. "You're not listening to her, are you? She's a lunatic!"

Delores laughs at her son's words. "It was all for money, dear. Charles collected the life insurance and everything from the estate and used it for their business."

Leo shakes his head. "Don't listen to her." He takes a step forward and I take another backwards. "Finish what you're saying, Delores."

"The deal was that if they needed more cash in the future, Leonard and I were next. Only my dear son had a change of heart. I made the mistake of telling him that his father made some changes to his will. I didn't realize that meant he took me out of it, but Leonard told me he included Leo in his inheritance again so that his son could get his 'fair share', as he called it."

Leo looks back at her. "Ten grand! Hardly my share." He looks back at me, his eyes full of rage. His demeanour softens when he sees the horror in my eyes. "This isn't what you think."

"It's much worse," Delores continues, looking at her son. "You and I talked one night, and I consoled you as you cried about how much your father hated you. I told you about him adding you to the will. You and your business partner decided that maybe you didn't have to kill both Leonard and I to collect the inheritance. Perhaps you could spare your dear mother. You had Charles kill your father. Staged it as a suicide. When you found out you would get peanuts, you went back to plan A, killing me as well." She laughs. "My own son," she says, tears falling freely now.

"That's not true!" Leo says, looking at his mother and back at me. "Don't listen to this garbage. She's trying to manipulate you, like she always does!"

Delores stands up slowly. "I'm not finished. You go out with your darling wife again. Set up for another perfect alibi. When I come back home, I rest. You instructed Charles to kill me that day, but he didn't expect to see Hannah. He murdered her, and it's all because of you."

I look back at Leo, confused. "You did this?"

He shakes his head. "Stop listening to her. She's crazy. You know that. How many times has she tried to set you up by manipulating me? She has been trying to ruin our marriage since she came here. I see that now. She begged me to stay here. I should have kicked her out the first night!"

Delores laughs. "Leo was the one who begged me to stay. I wanted to leave after the first night! He pleaded with me to stay so that he could help me. By help, he meant make it easier for him to kill me in his own home."

He shakes his head. "Stop lying! All you do is lie!" He looks back at me. "You know how she is."

"Stop gaslighting your wife, dear." She laughs and looks to me.

Leo sighs and takes a step towards me, breathing heavily. "Our life was better before she came. Let's have that life again. You hate her. You've told me. I hate her too. You see how it was living with her for a few days? Try doing it for half your life!"

Delores lowers her head. When she looks at me, she knows part of what Leo says is true. She shakes her head and undoes the top few buttons of her blouse, revealing her upper chest. "Finish the job, darling," she says to me. She laughs. "Just know that my fate will be yours one day."

I look back at Leo. "You killed Hannah."

My eyes narrow at my husband. Before I can aim the gun at him, he charges at me and grabs it from my hand, whipping me to the ground. Before he can fire, Delores jumps on his side, scratching his face, and he shouts. I get up and try to wrestle the shotgun away from my husband as he fights us both off.

He shoves me hard and aims the gun at his mother. On the stand beside me is the bronze statue of the Sterling family. I grab it and swing as hard as I can, striking Leo on the side of the head. He falls to the ground immediately.

Delores grabs the shotgun again, but Leo manages to hold the barrel.

"Let go!" she shouts. "Stop. Leo! It's over. Stop, son!"

He tries to wrestle it away from her and she pulls the trigger.

Leo falls backwards, dead before he hits the floor. Delores looks wide-eyed at him, and then at me. The barrel of the shotgun moves with her, until it's aimed at my chest. She takes several deep breaths. In the distance, I can hear sirens nearby. I'm not sure if they'll arrive on time to save me, though.

"Delores," I say calmly. Smoke rises from the barrel of the gun. I realize that she only has two shots, and she used one for Charles and the other Leo. The shotgun is empty.

She looks down at Leo and lowers the weapon, dropping it to the floor. She kneels beside her son, staining her designer clothes with his blood as she shrieks, "What have I done!"

CHAPTER 42

Please. Please.

I sit in my mother's bathroom, staring at the mirror, praying. I thought I wanted this, but after everything that's happened, being pregnant would be the worst thing imaginable.

I stare at the pregnancy test intensely, waiting for the results. No doubt as soon as I open the door, my mom will be waiting. She's just as anxious as I've been.

There was a time when having a child with Leo was everything I wanted. Each month when it didn't happen, I would cry in defeat that my womb was not with his child.

Everything is different now.

Leo was not the man I thought he was. He was a monster. I imagine what a child of his would be like. Oh god, what do I do if I'm pregnant? How could I look at this child without PTSD symptoms?

Thankfully, he wouldn't have a father like Leo to corrupt him. Leo's dead. His funeral was weeks ago. I've been at my mother's house ever since that traumatic night where I watched in horror as my husband nearly killed me.

Delores saved me. She killed her own son to do so. Imagine what it would be like to have your son try and kill you. And for what? Money? For his business with Charles.

I'm glad that after Leo's death, I walked away with nothing. I didn't want anything to do with his inheritance. Just like his father, Leo had loans that I didn't know about. After the sale of our mansion repaid the loans, there was nothing left. Even if there was, I don't think I'd have accepted it.

My life as a Sterling is over. I want nothing to do with my husband's family name. I've already started the paperwork to change my legal name back to my maiden one. The idea that I still share my husband's last name after what he tried to do makes me sick to my stomach.

If it wasn't for Delores, I'd have Leo's last name permanently etched on a tombstone. He likely would have murdered his mother next. Can't leave any witnesses. He needed the money for his business, after all. It was the whole reason he had his father killed and attempted to kill his mother.

Now the entire world knows what monsters Leo Sterling and Charles Rayer were. Two men who conspired to kill each other's parents to collect an inheritance and life insurance. By doing so, they would have the ultimate alibi.

Leo rigged the Rayers' vehicle so that they would have an accident. Charles killed my father-in-law. When it was discovered that Leo would get nothing from the will, he tried to kill his own mother next.

That didn't go as planned. Delores killed both the murderers.

I sometimes wonder what would have happened had Delores not intervened. What if I didn't come home that terrible night?

What if Leo was successful in murdering his mother? I would have continued to be married to the monster. The next time his business needed a cash injection, no doubt he would have looked to collect the life insurance he had on me.

My life has become a true crime story. I will never read this genre again after what I've been through.

I look down at the test strip and the results are revealed. There's no doubt about it. There are very few faulty pregnancy test results.

I step out of the bathroom, the test firmly in my hand. As I expected, my mom is waiting for me. Her face is just as concerned as mine was.

"So?" she asks, her eyebrows furrowed. When I don't answer, she assumes the worst. "It's okay. We'll figure it out."

"It's negative." I raise the test for her to see for herself. Tears begin to form in my eyes. "Negative," I repeat.

Mom hugs me. "Oh, my." She takes a deep breath. "We need to celebrate. Let's have some tea."

I laugh. "Not a huge celebration, but I'll take it." I try my best to collect myself when the doorbell rings and makes me jump.

Mom opens the door and greets the caller. She opens the door wider and Tony Cardone walks inside. "Thanks, ma'am," he says. He gives me a thin smile. "Madelyn, hello."

I give my own thin smile back. Immediately I notice his navy suit and gold colored watch on his wrist.

"New suit?" I ask.

"New suit for a new promotion," he says with a laugh. When he sees that I don't think he's funny, he apologizes. He takes a toothpick out of his pocket and places it in his mouth. "I tried to call you."

I point at him. "And I didn't answer for a reason."

He nods. "I get that, I do. I thought maybe you'd be at the funeral."

"For Leo? No way."

"I wasn't surprised, of course," Tony says, the toothpick loosely flopping between his lips. "I was surprised to see your former mother-in-law there though."

I lower my head. The idea is tragic. "Poor woman," I say, looking back at Tony. "She must be stricken with guilt."

I sometimes wonder whether if Delores had another shotgun shell in her weapon she would have used it on me. That night I thought so. Then again, I was in shock.

Cardone nods. "The police searched Charles Rayer's home, including his home office. I'm sure it's no surprise what the DPI of his printer is." He laughs.

I shake my head. "I really hope I never hear that word again. I may never own a printer ever."

Tony clears his throat. "I had to track you down," he says. "I wanted to give this to you myself. Cut through all the red tape." He hands me an envelope with my name on it. I open it slowly. "Your husband's life insurance policy. Your half."

I open the letter inside and feel dizzy when I see the one followed by multiple numbers after it.

EPILOGUE

Delores

I lie in the king size bed, completely satisfied in every way possible. The patio door to our resort room is open and I can hear the waves crashing on the beachfront. The sound soothes me into a more relaxed state than I already am.

My new husband comes out of the bathroom completely nude.

"Lunch?" Cero asks me.

"That sounds lovely, dear," I say. "We've certainly worked up an appetite."

We've had more sex in the past few days than I have fingers or toes. Our honeymoon adventure has been incredible. Initially I wanted to go to Fiji, but Cero talked me into going to Mexico. He said he wanted to visit some family. He doesn't talk about them very much, but now that I'm his wife, it only makes sense that I meet them officially.

I pray the encounter will go smoothly. I'm older than his mother by a few years. I can only imagine what they think.

My own friends believe I'm crazy for marrying a man in his twenties at my age. They don't understand how he makes me feel, though.

My own son tried to kill me for money. Leo successfully killed his father for money. Money. Money.

The things men do for it. I can understand the temptation of killing someone you don't care for if a check for millions is on the line, but to murder your own blood? That's not the son I raised. At least I thought so.

Now my son is gone, and it's because of me. He left me no choice in the matter. Had I not pulled the trigger, he would have. He would have killed me, and his wife.

Sometimes I think about Madelyn. I tried to snoop into her life through Facebook. She's not too active there and her security settings are tight so that is nearly impossible to see what she's been up to. Her mother, however, is less worried about such things. On her profile, there are many pictures of her and Madelyn. I believe the two are living together at the moment.

I don't blame her. She wants her mother to support her during what I imagine is a terrible time of recovery for her.

I, however, had no one to lean on, except Cero.

He was there for me in the hospital that terrible night that my son... He was with me for my son's funeral. I didn't care what anybody thought. Yes, I had an affair and he's with me at my son's funeral. I shouldn't be so worried about such matters. There weren't exactly very many people attending.

There were even fewer people at the funeral of Charles Rayer. I had Cero drive by his ceremony as I was curious. I spotted one elderly couple. It was his grandparents, I imagine. No one else was present.

Madelyn accused me of murdering two people at one time. In the end, I suppose she was right. Charles and my own son are buried six feet under because of me.

I look at my husband's naked body as he slowly puts clothes on while giving me a wicked smile. Despite the poorly working AC in the room, the humidity is close to unbearable. His body is glistening with sweat, making him even more appealing.

I smile to myself at how attractive my husband is. Leonard Sterling would be rolling in his grave if he could see me now and how happy I am.

I'm not stupid, though. I know what Cero and I have isn't exactly love. A lot of it is lust. Ever since I met Cero, I imagined what he would be like in bed and he was even better than I could ever have dreamt of.

I'm not sure why Cero married me. Money I'm sure has something to do with it, although I have much less now. Even with the sale of my home and the insurance money, my net worth is only a few million. I've had to make sacrifices, but I'm doing well.

Cero and I each made our own wills after getting married. I made sure mine was clear. My husband, Cero, gets everything. He's done the same, but for me. He doesn't exactly have much to inherit, though. He certainly won't be working as a landscaper now that he's my husband.

Cero looks at some paperwork on the desk in the room. "What's this?" he asks.

"Oh," I say, sitting up in bed, covering my body with the sheets. "I spoke with my lawyer before we left. I wanted us to finalize our life insurance. Just as talked about. If I was to die, which may be during this honeymoon, dear, with how fast you make my heart beat, the insurance money goes to you, and you alone. If you pass, your life insurance money will come to me." I give him a thin smile. I lower the cover and reveal my breasts, taking his attention away from the paperwork for a moment. "Hurry up, dear. I need more attention from my husband."

"Esparer, esparer," he says, pleading with me to wait. I love his accent. I light a cigarette as he signs the paperwork and quickly gets into the sheets with me.

Love fades in most relationships over time. Lust goes away even quicker. Money isn't everything in life. If I've learned anything about what happened with my son and I, I know that much. I blow out a plume of smoke as I stare deep into Cero's sultry eyes.

Money isn't everything, but I also learned a lot during my marriage with Leonard Sterling. When your marriage eventually has no love or lust, more money is good to have.

❋ ❋ ❋

Note from the author:

I truly hope you enjoyed reading my story as much as I did creating it. As an indie author, what you think of my book is all I care about.
If you enjoyed my story, please take a moment to leave your review on the Amazon store. It would mean the world to me.
Thank you for reading, and I hope you join me next time.

Sincerely,

James

Download My Free Book

If you would like to receive a FREE copy of my psychological thriller, The Affair, please email me at jamescaineauthor@gmail.com.

Thanks again,
James

And now please enjoy a short excerpt from my book, Mother and Daughter:

❖ ❖ ❖

MOTHER AND DAUGHTER

Her mother's rules were simple, but Annie Meadows rarely followed them.

The rules were required though if they didn't want to get caught.

Sometimes Annie believed what she and her mother did was wrong, but she was told they were helping the children in the basement. When Annie heard them cry in their locked rooms, it didn't feel that way.

As she got older, Annie reflected on what she had done and vowed to never be like her mother. Then she met little Gracie Bradshaw, a child in her daycare classroom. Gracie is special, just like Annie was.

Now, Annie wants to help the little girl, and the only way she knows how is with her **mothers' rules.**

PROLOGUE
Before

Mother says we're helping the children in the basement. Sometimes it doesn't feel that way.

When I hear their small voices and the others crying, some asking for help, I wonder if Mother is right.

"Ms. Annie Meadows!" Mother calls out to me from the kitchen. I stand from the living room table.

"Yes," I say as I approach her cautiously.

She's standing over the stove, a spatula firmly in her hand. She nods her head towards a plate of food.

"If you would, my darling child," she says to me with a smile, "please, give this to room one."

"Okay, Mother," I say, giving her my own smile back.

She raises the spatula. "And," she says, "do not speak to room two. You promised me you would stop. I know you did last night."

How did she know? I wasn't loud. They were scared and lonely. They needed someone to talk to. I like to think I help people too, better than Mother does.

I continue to stare up at my mother, and the spatula over her head. Her smile fades. "Now, little girl, please do as I say. Hurry, before their food gets cold. And—"

"I won't speak to them," I complete her sentence for her.

"Good," she says. "Now, after lunch, we're going to start our reading period."

I grab the plate and start walking down the narrow basement stairs.

I love reading. I love learning.

Sometimes I wish I could be more like the other children I see from my bedroom window. When Mother gets ready for the day, I watch the kids scurry down the block to get to school on time. On nice days, Mother allows me to read outside on the porch, where I can hear the sounds of nearby schoolchildren playing outside at recess.

They'll yell and scream their heads off for some reason, and I wonder what could be happening to them.

I hear yelling from the basement, but it's different.

Mother teaches me at home. She tells me I'm smarter this way. I'm special. Not like the other children. I have a deeper purpose than the children I hear outside.

Sometimes though, I wish I was just like the other kids. I wish I could scream with them from the playground.

One time I asked my mother if I could go to school like the other children.

She did not like that question.

She said it was important for us to stay home. What we did with the people in the basement was special.

Nobody but us could do it.

Mother made me promise to never tell a soul what she does. They wouldn't understand. They wouldn't see it as helping the children.

Mother says that after they leave our home, they're different. Better.

Changed.

We're making them whole again.

I've never seen the children after they leave to ask, but I wish I could. I want to know how much better their lives are. I want to know how happy they are after staying with us.

I want to tell the voice inside me that questions Mother that what I help her do is helping them.

As I get to the basement, I hear muffled sounds coming from one of the rooms. I walk past a bookshelf, where we hide the hole that leads to the special hallway where we keep them.

Inside are two rooms. Each has a heavy door that Mother has to help me unlock and open.

Both rooms have a metal slot at the bottom of the door. I open it, and place the plate of food inside room one.

"Thank you," a little girl's voice says.

I do as Mother asks and don't speak to them. She's likely upstairs listening. She's likely testing me to see if I'll do as she asked.

I may be only seven years old, but I know to follow what Mother says.

I close the slot and look down the small hallway at room two. The muffled sounds continue to come from it.

The sounds of crying.

Mother says we're helping them. It doesn't feel that way.

CHAPTER 1

Sarah
Present

Report Domestic Abuse.

I stare at the signage in my doctor's office as I wait in the lobby for my prescription.

I think of my husband, Roger. Last night was not a good one. This morning too. I wish I could go back in time and stop our fight from getting worse.

De-escalate Roger and get him to cool off before he exploded.

Worse, it all happened in front of Gracie. She's only four years old but knows that daddy gets angry sometimes.

It scared her. She doesn't understand. She doesn't see what led up to our fight. I took things too far. I should have backed off, knowing that Roger was going to be upset.

Instead, I made things worse. I yelled at him. Said things I regret.

Roger didn't like that. His voice started to raise and match mine, and soon after he was flat-out yelling.

Things got worse.

It was only when I saw the frightened face of my little girl that I worried about it.

I saw my father and mother fight when I was young.

That was as normal as Tuesday coming after Monday. Father would yell, but unlike me, my mother just took it. She never did so much as whimper back to him. That didn't stop my father from starting arguments.

Father was a shorter man. Not really intimidating for his size. Even as a child, I thought he was frail. I would yell back at him continuously. Rebel child, my mother called me.

Not her. She was the complete opposite. Fully submissive.

Whatever my dad said, she did. Whatever Father commanded, she followed.

At least Roger is different. He certainly is many things, but he's not like my dad. That much I got right when I married him.

The fight last night bothers me, though. I wonder what Gracie is thinking. What her little mind is construing to make sense of it all.

I sigh, and the doctor comes into the small waiting room. "Hey, Sarah," she says with a smile. "Sorry for the wait. Our printer stopped working and I had to use my non-existent tech skills to fix it to print this off." She hands me the prescription. "I know you're worried about the side effects of taking Prozac, but I know this will help things. It's also a very low dose. We can put you on this medication to help, okay?"

I look around the empty room and sigh, knowing that nobody, not even the receptionist who's not at her desk, heard what the doctor said. I don't want to take drugs. My doctor says I have depression. It doesn't feel that way. I still can be with my child and take care of the house. Sure, I'm more tired, but I can still live my life every day.

Functional depression, my doctor calls it.

I grab the prescription and thank her again before leaving.

I'm not sure if I'll actually get the prescription filled. My doctor talked me into taking it from her after reviewing how it could help me. She didn't exactly pressure me, but she didn't exactly let me say no.

I didn't come to her clinic for depression. We were just to review a recent ultrasound I had. Somehow I came for the test on my shoulder and walked out with a prescription for Prozac.

How did that happen?

I take out my phone and notice the time.

I hurry to my car and start it, knowing I'll be late picking up Gracie from daycare again.

Last time the office said they would charge me if I continued to be late. Maybe I can tell them I have functional depression and to give me a break, but somehow I know that won't make things better. Besides, I'd rather not tell anyone.

The supervisor of the daycare, an older lady named Mabel, explained it was just policy to start charging per minute parents are late picking up their children.

That would be great.

Roger would certainly be happier having to pay extra for me being late picking up our child. Especially since he never wanted her to be in daycare to begin with. He'd rather I take care of her at home.

Being with other children at her age is important, though. She needs more than just me or Grandma to play with. Now that I want to go back to a job, we can hopefully afford it.

Thankfully, living in a smaller city has its perks. It's easy to get to anywhere quickly. Esta is the one of the smallest cities in the province of Alberta, Canada.

It has that small town appeal, but with a Walmart.

I park in the lot of a strip mall. When I get out, I can still hear some of the children playing from the gated area where the daycare is.

Their voices make me smile, knowing I can't be too late if other children are there.

I slow and see two little girls playing hopscotch behind the gated area. They're having fun, laughing almost in unison.

Gracie is standing in the corner, alone. She's not doing anything as far as I can tell but look at the brick wall of the daycare. She kicks a stone and watches it fly past the gate.

I wish she would play with other children. She reminds me so much of myself when I was younger. I tended to be alone. Not much has changed now that I'm an adult. I never really had many friends, even in high school. A few, enough to get by, but I had always thought Gracie would be better.

I had hoped she wouldn't be like me.

How could she be any more outgoing with me as her mother?

It's not like we take her out to friends' homes so she can play with their children. Roger and I don't go out often. We're always together, as a family.

We call it family time, and we love having it, but I wish we had more friends. I've heard it's easier to make friends as parents. You bring your child somewhere and if they start playing with other kids, you chat with their parents. Just as easily as your child has made a new friend, so have you.

What if your child stays to themselves though? What

if the child's parents aren't outgoing either? I'm not. At least Roger is very different.

Why couldn't Gracie have taken after him more?

I worry how Gracie will be when she starts kindergarten next year. I remember how it felt playing alone at recess when I was her age. I remember how shy I was. How much I wanted other kids to ask me to play, and how scared I was to approach other kids to play with them.

Gracie's face lights up when she spots me. "Mommy!" she calls out. She puts her hands on the gate and shakes it as if she has the strength to break through.

"Hey, Gracie," I say with my own wide smile. "Did you have a good day?"

"Can we go home?" she asks, ignoring the question.

"Hey, Mrs. Bradshaw." My daughter's daycare teacher, Annie Meadows, walks up to me. Her flowing dress moves wildly with the breeze. I notice the small cartoon hearts printed at the bottom of it. She always has some type of weird dress like that. Gracie tells me what Ms. Meadows wore at daycare whenever I ask her how her day was at home.

Annie pats Gracie's head. "Gracie had a great day today," she says in her usual polite voice.

"Hey, Annie," I say. "That's great to hear." I look down at Gracie. "Can me and Ms. Meadows talk for a moment, dear? Maybe go play on the swing."

Gracie nods and is about to leave when Annie kneels so that she's at eye level with my daughter.

"Please give me and your mother a minute," she says to Annie, repeating what I had just asked Gracie to do. It slightly irritates me but it's hard to stay mad at such an odd young woman.

All the children love Ms. Meadows at daycare; she has a way with them. Gracie always tells me stories about what she did that day. She comes off so awkward and proper to me, though.

Gracie runs towards the swing and sits on it, looking back up at me. "Mommy, can you push me?"

I smile. "I just need a minute to talk to Ms. Meadows, okay? Just swing yourself."

"Is everything okay, Ms. Bradshaw?" Annie asks.

"Please, just call me Sarah," I remind her. I've said it so many times, but Annie is not one to skip formalities.

"Mommy!" Gracie yells, sitting on the swing, not moving, "I don't know how."

I sigh. "Honey, just give me one minute, okay?"

Gracie pouts and sits on the swing, not moving, except to sway a little under gravity.

"Sorry," I say to Annie. I look back at Gracie a moment before continuing. "I'm just worried about her."

"What about?"

"I worry that she's not playing with other children as much as she should."

Annie gives a thin smile. "Gracie is an exceptional child. You really are a lucky mother."

"Thanks, Annie." I smile. "She is, I know. I just worry that she doesn't show much interest in speaking to other children, let alone playing with them."

Annie nods. "I understand. Every child comes into their own social time when it makes sense for them. I'm not worried about her. I was like her when I was younger myself. I had a hard time playing with children, but now I play with them all day."

I smile, but her answer is strange. "Thanks, Annie, I'm sure I'm worried about nothing."

I call Gracie to come and leave with me, and thank Annie again before we do. My daughter holds my hand as we walk into the parking lot.

When we're close to my car, I see several young girls playing at the playground across the street.

I smile while looking down at my daughter. "Hey, I have an idea. How about we play at the playground for a little while?"

Gracie looks across the street, at the children playing, but doesn't answer.

"Come on," I say. "It'll be fun." I point at the empty swing set. "I'll push you this time." Gracie smiles and nods in agreement.

Before I start to push her, I quickly text Roger to let him know that we're at the park beside the daycare.

Gracie and I are having fun, mostly because of my hard labor pushing her. After what feels like an eternity, I stop and tell Gracie that Mommy needs a break.

"Can we just go home now?" she asks.

I look at the three little girls playing near the slide, and the two mothers sitting across from them chatting to each other.

"How about you play for a little more on the slide for a bit? Then, I promise we'll go home." Gracie doesn't seem enthralled. "And if you have fun playing, we'll have ice cream after dinner today!"

That does the trick. Gracie smiles and runs towards the slide where the other children are playing. Instead of talking to them, though, she pours rocks down the slide, making it so the other kids can't go down. I roll my eyes.

I remind Gracie to play nice since others want to use the slide too. One of the two mothers on the bench smiles at me and waves.

I smile back. "Hi," I say to them. Only one of them greets me back.

I go back to the bench I was sitting at across from the mothers and watch Gracie play. After a while, a miracle happens. Gracie is actually talking to one of the little girls at the playground. Soon enough, she joins the others in playing. They sit together on the playground rocks, talking amongst themselves.

I smile. I need to do more of this with Gracie.

She's actually getting along with other children. I think about approaching the other mothers and introducing myself. I can't help but think how one of them didn't greet me back. Maybe they want to be left alone.

As I watch Gracie play with the kids, though, I wonder if I should say something. Isn't this the part where I speak to the children's parents? Ask them questions? Maybe even a number to arrange for a playdate?

Or is that weird?

It all seems so forward.

Before I can make up my mind, I spot my husband's red car coming down the block and parking on the street.

CHAPTER 2

Roger

I stare at the different colored flower bouquets. Which one best represents how crappy a person I feel right now?

Which type of flower tells my wife how sorry I am for last night?

What can I give her so she'll forget the man I was yesterday and remember how I usually am?

A woman who works at the grocery store sees me looking at the flower selection, completely lost. "Can I help you?" she asks.

I take in a breath. She's a young pretty girl. Maybe only nineteen. I remember at her age I used to buy flowers for pretty girls all the time. It was something I charmed them with that they were not used to.

I liked to think that I had "game," as the kids call it these days. A way with women where I could romanticize them into my arms. Flowers always set a nice standard for what they could expect from me.

Now, I'm getting older. I married a pretty girl but haven't given her flowers in a long time.

All I've given her is grief.

"Well," I tell the young woman, "I'm sort of in the doghouse with my wife."

She laughs. "You did have the look of trouble, so I wondered."

I nod with a thin smile. "If I upset you beyond belief, which flowers would you want to receive that could make it so you hate me just a smidge less?"

She shakes her head. "I don't know what your wife likes. Does she have a preference?"

Good question. I don't remember buying her anything in over a decade. I remember when I was younger, I used to know which color represented what emotion. Red was a little too sexy for an apology flower. Implied romance or lust. Not what Sarah likely had in mind for me tonight.

I need a flower that says I'm raising the white flag. I come in peace. I'm not here to fight, and I surrender.

I look at some pretty light pink roses. "You know what, I'll just grab these ones," I say confidently. The cashier nods and wraps them up for me.

When I get to my car, my phone vibrates. I put the bouquet on top of my car and look. It's Sarah letting me know she's at the playground near the daycare.

I don't want to wait for Sarah and Gracie to come back home to tell her how sorry I am. Maybe a visit to the park with my family is the perfect set-up. A good way to reunite with my wife and daughter after last night.

I haven't had a chance to talk to Gracie since my little blow-up yesterday.

I get inside my car and turn on the ignition. It starts as quickly as my rage the other day.

What hurts me most when I think of it is the look on Gracie's face. I remember having that look myself as a boy. Mom and Dad would fight, only he would take things too far.

The first time he struck my mom, I wanted to kill him. Had I not been seven years old, I would have tried. I remember, when my parents were asleep, I snuck into the kitchen and opened the drawer, taking out a large kitchen knife.

He hurt my mom. He was the one who needed to be hurt. What had she done to deserve his wrath? I don't even remember now that I'm an adult. All I do remember was holding that knife, thinking what I should do to him.

It was crazy, I know. I wanted to protect my mom, even if it was from my own father. That wasn't the last time he hit her. It was only when I got older that I challenged him once.

We fought, and I won.

I remember how good it felt, standing over my dad, collapsed on the floor after I smashed him in the face.

He understood who the new man of the house was.

It was better for Mom after that. I'm not sure what changed inside my father, but he never hit her again.

We continued to act as a family, despite our past. We didn't have very many loving times. Eventually I moved out, and he passed away. Mother now lives in a small apartment a few hours away from Esta. We visit her when we can.

It's only been a few months since my dad died. I know I should give myself a break about what happened last night with Sarah. I'm not myself.

My father's funeral wasn't too long ago. As much as I tell myself I don't care about that, I do. It's... complicated.

Still, the look on Gracie's little face gets to me.

I continue to drive to the playground, wondering how I'm ever going to make things up not only to my wife, but my daughter as well.

I look at the bouquet in the passenger seat.

How many times did my father attempt to make things right after he destroyed something?

Never.

How many flowers did he buy my mom?

None.

I'm not him, I remind myself.

I take responsibility for what I've done, and we'll make this right.

How do I make right what I haven't told her yet, though? What will Sarah's reaction be when I tell her I've been lying to her? When she finds out what I've been up to, how many flowers can I buy her to make up for that?

She'll find out eventually, most likely soon.

I can't keep hiding it.

One battle at a time, I remind myself. I have to get through this before I can tell her everything.

I sigh, wondering, what have I done? I'm not myself, though. I haven't been making good decisions lately.

We've had darker moments than this. Six months ago, I thought she would leave me for sure. She should have.

I would have if I were her.

She didn't, though, and things did get better, until recently.

I spot the playground ahead and smile, noticing Gracie playing with other kids. Sarah and I have been worried about her social skills. I've continued to tell her not to worry about it. She'll get more exposure to other kids as she continues with daycare and starts grade school.

Seeing Gracie play makes me smile.

When I park on the street beside the playground, I see

the look of concern Sarah has as she glances at me.

My smile fades as I remember what a piece of garbage I really am.

❋ ❋ ❋